His hands burned as he touched her everywhere. His lips were set afire by her kisses.

"I want you, Jericho," she whispered against his mouth. "I feel alive with you. What's between us is right. I know you feel it, too. Show me. Please."

The sound of her urgent plea knocked the sense back into his muddled brain.

He gently took her by the shoulders and set her back from him. "This isn't right." He eased her up into his arms and slid her into the pickup's front seat.

Striding around the cab, he slipped behind the wheel and started it up. "You must belong to someone—somewhere. If we give in tonight and tomorrow your memory comes back, you'll never forgive yourself—or me. I won't take that chance."

Dear Reader,

Instead of a letter and a dedication for this book, I've decided to combine the two.

To the five other fabulous authors who worked with me to create this THE COLTONS: FAMILY FIRST series: Marie, Beth, Caridad, Justine and Carla—you guys rock!

To Patience Smith, our editor extraordinaire: thanks for putting up with us and letting us share this ride into Texas and the Colton family. It was great fun.

And to all readers of the Coltons: writing *The Sheriff's Amnesiac Bride* was definitely a labor of love for me. Thanks for picking up this book and joining our world. Enjoy!

Happy Reading,

Linda

LINDA CONRAD

The Sheriff's Amnesiac Bride

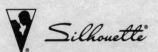

Romantic
SUSPENSE

Special thanks and acknowledgment to
Linda Conrad for her contribution to
THE COLTONS: FAMILY FIRST miniseries.

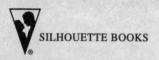 SILHOUETTE BOOKS

ISBN-13: 978-0-373-27606-6
ISBN-10:   0-373-27606-0

THE SHERIFF'S AMNESIAC BRIDE

Visit Silhouette Books at www.eHarlequin.com

Printed in U.S.A.

LINDA CONRAD

was inspired by her mother, who gave her a deep love of storytelling. "Mom told me I was the best liar she ever knew. That's saying something for a woman with an Irish storyteller's background," Linda says. Winner of many awards, including the *Romantic Times BOOKreviews* Reviewers' Choice and a Maggie, Linda has often appeared on the Waldenbooks and BookScan bestseller lists. Her favorite pastime is finding true passion in life. Linda, her husband and KiKi, the dog, work, play, live and love in the sunshine of the Florida Keys. Visit Linda's Web site at www.LindaConrad.com.

Chapter 1

Uh-oh. Big trouble.

"Shut up, lady." One of the two men in the front seat swung his arm over the seat back and smacked her across the cheek. "You're in no spot to argue. You say you can't remember? Well, that ain't my problem."

The driver didn't turn around, but muttered, "When we get back, the boss'll make you talk. And he won't be as nice as we are. You took something that didn't belong to you, and that's a no-no."

"But...but I really can't remember." She rubbed at her stinging cheek. "I don't even know who I am." Tears welled up and she fought the panic that was quickly crawling up her spine. She didn't dare cry. Hardly dared to breathe.

Caught in an internal struggle for clarity, she'd been trying to bring up memories from her past. She was desperate to remember anything at all. Even her own name escaped her, and it had been this way for what seemed like hours.

Where there should've been something, there was a huge void. Darkness. A little pain. But nothing even vaguely familiar.

She didn't have a clue as to why these men had forced her into the backseat of this speeding car. Or where on earth they were heading. Everything out the window seemed as alien as everything in her mind. She didn't know what she was doing here. Or who these horrible men were who kept insisting she tell them where "it" was.

The only thing she did know was that these two goons were carrying guns. Big ones. They'd waved them at her when she tried to tell them she couldn't remember.

Oh, God, help her. She was going to die if something didn't give soon.

Putting her hands together, she silently prayed for a break. Some way of escaping this car and these two men.

As if God had answered her prayer directly, a church spire appeared out the front windshield. The car slowed.

"What the hell is all this traffic about?" The driver sounded irritated as he slammed his foot on the brake. "It ain't Sunday, damn it. Get out of our way, you idiots!"

Oh please, let me find a way out, she silently begged. Let this be the time. Let this be a place where I can find sanctuary and someone who will save a desperate woman with no memory.

Then, quietly, an answer came to her from out of the emptiness in her mind. *The Lord helps those who help themselves.*

Sheriff Jericho Yates glanced up toward the Esperanza Community Church steps looming directly ahead and slowed his pace. He wasn't chickening out of his own wedding, but there was truly no sense in getting there before the bride-to-be would be ready to start.

"You're sure you want to go through with this, bro?" Fisher, his older brother and the best man, slowed his steps too.

With a serious face but eyes that always seemed to be laughing behind his sunglasses, Fisher Yates, U.S. Army captain home on leave, rarely showed any emotion. But at the moment, it was Fisher who looked panic-stricken by the thought of this wedding.

"Hell, yes, I'm going through with it," Jericho muttered as an answer. "I gave Macy my word. But I don't want to piss her off by showing up too soon. We've been best friends ever since I can remember, and I couldn't hurt her feelings by embarrassing her like that."

"Well, I remember when there were three of you best friends—back in the day. You and Macy and Tim Ward. I thought the whole idea of two guys and a gal hanging out and being so close was a little weird at the time. And sure enough, it was Macy and Tim that eventually got hitched. So what were *you* all those years? The dorky third wheel?"

Jericho straightened his shoulders under the weight of his rented tux and rammed his hands into his pockets. He would not let Fisher get to him today. His slightly shorter big brother, who was only just now back from his third tour of duty in the Middle East, could be a pain in the ass. But Jericho felt he needed to make allowances for Fisher—for possible psychological problems. Or whatever.

He opened his mouth to remind Fisher that the three of them, he and Tim and Fisher, too, had all been half in love with Macy in high school. But then, Jericho thought better of jamming the truth in his brother's face right now. Tim had been the one to win the prize. Jericho also remembered that Fisher had taken off in a hurry to join the army after Macy picked Tim to marry—and his brother had never looked back once.

"No," Jericho finally answered, forcing a grin. "I was the best friend and glad about my buddies hooking up and being happy together. I was also the friend who stood by Macy when Tim got sick and died six years ago. And today, I'm the friend who's going to marry her and give Tim's teenage son a new father."

"Yeah, you are. And right friendly of you, too, bro. But as you said earlier, you and Macy aren't in love. What's the real deal? I'm not buying this friendly daddy-stand-in story."

Jericho wasn't sure he could explain it to someone like Fisher, a guy who'd never had anybody depending on him—except, of course, for the men in his squad. Well, okay, his brother probably would understand loyalty and honor, but not when it came to women or kids or best friends. Fisher had never let any of those things into his life.

"The real story is that I'm not *in* love with Macy…."

"You said that already."

"But…I do love her and want the best for her. And that kid of hers and Tim's already seems like family to me. I'm his godfather, and I think I can make a bigger difference to his life as his stepfather. I mean to try."

T.J. was the foremost reason Jericho had been so determined to go through with this wedding when Macy had brought up the subject. As kids, Fisher and he had done without a mother after theirs had abandoned them. But they'd had the firm hand of a father to raise them right. As a tribute to his dad, Buck Yates, still by far the best father in the world, Jericho would bring T.J. into the family and do for him what Buck had done for his two sons. Give T.J. the greatest start possible.

"Act like a best man, why don't you, and just shut up about love and real stories." He poked Fisher lightly on his dress-uniformed arm. "We need to waste a few more minutes out here, bro. If you've gotta keep yakking at me, tell me what your plans are for after your leave is over."

Just inside the Community Church, waiting behind closed doors in the vestibule with her maid of honor, Macy Ward fidgeted with her dress. "What do you think everyone in town will have to say about me wearing off-white? Maybe I should've worn a light blue dress instead."

The dress was of no consequence, but Macy didn't want to say what she really had on her mind. Her maid of honor, Jewel Mayfair, was also her boss. And although she really liked Jewel, being too honest in a case like this might not be the best idea. Even though Macy was about to be married, she still needed the job.

So as devastated as she felt by the nasty looks she'd received from Jericho's brother at the rehearsal last night, and as much as she would love to pour her heart out to another woman as kind as Jewel, she would instead keep her mouth firmly shut on the subject of Fisher Yates. Anyway, he was about to become her brother-in-law. So the two of them would just have to find a way of getting along.

But Macy felt nervous and jittery about more than just an irritating old boyfriend in uniform. She was dwelling on something much more important. Her son T.J. had been giving her fits over this upcoming marriage. He'd said he didn't want anyone to take his father's place. Though her boy liked Jericho well enough, and eventually Macy felt sure he would come to love and respect the man as much as the rest of the town.

What was not to love? Jericho Yates was the best man she knew. He was kind, loyal and so honest it almost hurt her heart. His honesty had recently made her feel guilty because she had not been absolutely honest with him or anyone else in such a long time.

"What's wrong, Macy? You don't look happy. You should be ecstatic. Today's your wedding day."

"I'm okay, Jewel. Honest. It's just…" She decided to confide in her boss, at least a little. "Jericho and I aren't in love. Not like a man and woman who are about to be married are supposed to be."

"No? But then why get married?"

"My son." Macy plopped down in the nearest chair, disregarding the possible wrinkles to her dress. "T.J. needs a father badly. And Jericho will make such a great dad. I'm the one who convinced our poor county sheriff to take pity on an old friend and do me the honor. I knew he would never tell me no."

"But now you're having second thoughts?"

"Second, third and fourth thoughts actually. I'm about to ruin a good man's life and saddle him with a wife he doesn't love and a kid who's a handful.

"I like Jericho," she added hastily. "A lot. I don't know if I can do this to him."

Jewel knelt on the carpet beside Macy's chair and spoke quietly. "If you ask me, he'll be getting the best part of the deal. You don't seem to understand how really beautiful and special you are, and I'm not sure why you don't get it. You're a terrific mother and a fine employee. I'm both your boss and your maid of honor, a double threat at the moment. So I'm the one who's here to remind you of what everyone else already knows. If you decide not to go through with this wedding, it'll be Jericho's loss, not yours."

Macy's eyes clouded over with unshed tears, but she bit them back. Jewel had become the dearest friend. But when everything was said and over, Macy just could not go through with this sham wedding. At least not today.

"Jewel, will you back me up if I postpone the wedding?"

Jewel put an arm around her shoulders. "Sure, honey. But why don't you go out and talk to Jericho about it first? Maybe you can catch him on his way in."

"Come with me?"

"All right. But we'd better hurry. The guests are already arriving. There's a major traffic jam outside."

* * *

Outside under the cottonwoods and next to the church, standing with his brother Fisher beside him, Jericho had been biding his time. He turned when he heard someone calling his name.

"Sheriff Yates!" The voice was coming from his deputy Adam Rawlins.

Jericho watched as the man he'd hired not long ago hurried toward him. Adam was dressed in his full deputy's uniform because he'd been on duty today and hadn't planned on attending the wedding. Rawlins was a good man who had come to them with terrific references from a deputy job in Wyoming. And Jericho was mighty glad to have found him.

"Sheriff, we've got ourselves a traffic tie-up out here on the highway. Someone called it in and I thought I'd better come over and direct traffic."

Geez. The entire county must be planning on attending his wedding. Who all had Macy invited? He'd left the plans up to her because he'd been so busy for the last few weeks. What with that case of identity theft a while back and then an actual dead body and a murder investigation out on Clay Colton's ranch that had just been put to bed, the sheriff's business was booming lately.

"All right, deputy," he told Rawlins. "Thanks for the quick thinking. I'll be out of pocket here for a few more hours and then I can help you out."

The deputy nodded and raced back toward the highway, apparently all ready to set out traffic cones and organize traffic lanes.

"Aren't you and Macy going on a honeymoon, bro?"

Fisher laid a hand on Jericho's arm, reminding him of his presence and of the upcoming nuptials.

Jericho winced and shook his head. "Not funny, bubba. You already know the answer to that. Besides, Macy and I are planning on spending some quality time with T.J. over the next few days. I thought I might take him hunting like Dad used to do for us. I hear the wild boar hunting has been good up on the north Gage pasture."

"Yeah, wild boar hunting the day after your wedding does sound romantic." Fisher scowled and rolled his eyes.

Jericho shook off his brother's sarcastic comments. He didn't care what Fisher or anybody thought of this marriage to his best friend. Macy was a great lady and a great friend, and Jericho vowed to do right by her and her son—regardless of anyone else's opinion.

Still twisting her hands in the backseat and waiting for a good opportunity, the woman with no past and a questionable future bit her lip and stared out the car's window. There was so much traffic here. Surely one of the people in these other cars would see her predicament and come to her aid.

"Son of a bitch, the traffic's even worse now." The car wound down to a crawl as the driver turned around again to speak to her. "Don't get smart, lady. You call out or make any noises like you need help and we'll shoot you. I don't give a rat's damn if that special item the boss wants is ever found or not. The choice between you giving us the answer and you never being able to answer again ain't nothing to me.

"You got that?"

She nodded, but the movement seared a line of fiery pain down her temple. Another couple of pains like that and she might rather be dead anyway.

"Terrific," the goon sitting shotgun said. "Just look at that, will ya? A local smoky. Out in the middle of the highway, directing traffic. Crap.

"What's going to happen, Arnie?" The man in the passenger seat was beginning to sweat.

"We're not doing anything wrong," Arnie answered with a growl. "We're regular citizens just driving down the road. Nothing to worry about. Stash your gun under the seat until we pass him by."

The driver bent and buried his own gun, then twisted back to her. "Remember, sis. No funny stuff. I swear, if you call out, you're dead."

Shaking badly, she wondered if her voice would work anyway. But right then, the miracle she'd prayed for happened. Their car came to a complete stop, almost directly in front of the church.

She bit her lip and tried to guess whether it would be closer for her to head for the sanctuary of the church or to run for the policeman in the street ten car-lengths away. The truck in front of them inched ahead and she decided to break for the church—it was her only real choice.

For a split second she stopped to wonder if she might be the kind of person who made rash decisions and who would rather fight back than die with a whimper. But then, whether out of fear or out of instinct, she knew it didn't matter.

If she were ever going to find out what had happened to her in the first place, she would have to go. Now.

* * *

Jericho heard a popping sound behind his back. Spinning around, he scanned the area trying to make out where the noise had originated.

"Was that a gunshot?" Fisher asked, as he too checked out the scene in front of the church.

In his peripheral vision, Jericho spotted a woman he'd never seen before. A woman seemingly out of place for a wedding, dressed in fancy jeans and red halter top. And she was racing at top speed across the grass straight in his direction. What the hell?

Another pop and the woman fell on the concrete walkway. From off to his left, someone screamed. Then tires squealed from somwhere down the long line of cars. When he glanced toward the sound, he saw a sedan with two men sitting in front as they roared out of the line and headed down the narrow shoulder of the highway.

Chaos reigned. Car horns honked. People shouted. And the sedan spewed out a huge dust plume as it bumped down the embankment.

Jericho took off at a run. He dropped to one knee beside the woman, checked her pulse and discovered she was breathing but unconscious and bleeding.

"Is she alive?" Deputy Rawlins asked, almost out of breath as he came running up. "I got their plates, Sheriff. But I didn't dare get off a shot with all the civilians in the way. You want me to pursue?"

Son of a gun. It would figure that he didn't have his weapon just when an emergency arose.

"Stay with the woman," Jericho ordered. "You and

Fisher get her to Doc O'Neal's as fast as you can. My rifle's in the truck, and…" He looked over his shoulder toward the church door. "Tell Macy…"

Right then Macy appeared at the top of the church steps and peered down at him. He was about to yell for her to get back out of the line of fire. But within a second, he could see her quickly taking in the whole situation.

"You go do what you need to, Jericho," she called out to him. "Don't worry about us. Just take care of yourself. The wedding's off for today."

Chapter 2

It was one of those spectacular Texas sunsets, but Jericho had been too preoccupied to enjoy it. Now that the sun had completely dropped below the horizon, he retraced his steps to the Community Church and the pre-arranged meeting with his deputy.

"Sorry you didn't catch them, Sheriff. I searched the grounds like you told me when you called in, and I came up with just this one bullet casing. From a 9mm. Pretty common, I'm afraid."

Jericho felt all of his thirty-five years weighing heavily on his shoulders tonight. "Yeah, but just in case there might be anything special, send it off to the lab in San Antonio. Okay?" It wasn't often that a trained lawman witnessed an attempted murder and couldn't either catch—or identify—the perpetrators. So why him? And why on his wedding day?

The deputy nodded and put the plastic evidence bag back into his jacket pocket.

"What happened with the victim?" Jericho asked wearily. "Is she still alive?"

"Last time I checked she was sitting up and able to talk, still over at Doc O'Neal's clinic. But she wasn't giving many answers."

That figured. Why make his job any easier?

"Did you run the plates?"

Deputy Rawlins frowned. "Stolen. Not the car. The plates were stolen in San Marcos day before yesterday."

Jericho's frustration grew but he kept it hidden as he rolled up the sleeves of his starched, white dress shirt. "When I checked in the last time, everyone else was okay. That still true?" He was concerned about Macy. How had she handled postponing the wedding?

"I never saw an assemblage of people disband so quickly or so quietly." The deputy removed his hat and fiddled with the brim. "Mrs. Ward was amazing. Once we were sure the immediate danger was over, she told everyone to go home and that she'd notify them when there would be another try at the wedding. Had everybody chuckling pretty good…but they went."

"I'd better call her."

"Yes, sir." With a tired sigh, Deputy Rawlins flipped his hat back onto his head. "Doc O'Neal needs someone to take charge of the woman victim. Says her condition is not serious enough to send her over to the Uvalde hospital, but she isn't capable of being on her own, either. You want me to handle it, Sheriff?"

"No, Adam. You've had a long day and you've done a fine job. You go on home. I'll clean up the odds and ends."

The deputy nodded and turned, but then hesitated and turned back. "Sorry about the wedding, boss. Don't you think that whole shooting scene was really odd for broad daylight? What do you suppose it was all about?"

When Jericho just raised his eyebrows and didn't answer, Adam continued, "Wait 'til you try to question that woman victim. She's a little odd, too. Wouldn't say much to me. But she's sure something terrific to look at."

"Thanks. Good-night now." Jericho would talk to the victim, and he would take charge of her and this case. But he had a mighty tough phone call to Macy to make first.

As Jericho stepped into Dr. O'Neal's clinic, his shoulders felt a thousand times lighter. Macy had been wonderful on the phone—as usual. She'd tried hard to make him feel better about ruining the wedding. She had even told him that she'd been considering postponing anyway. When he asked her why such a thing would occur to her, she said they would talk tomorrow.

In a way, he was curious and wondered if he'd done something inadvertent, other than being the sheriff, to make her mad. But in another way, his whole body felt weightless. He had meant to marry Macy today. Still did, in fact. He'd given his word. Besides that, recently he'd come to the conclusion that it was important for him to become a family man in order to honor his father.

But before Macy had suggested it a couple of weeks

ago, he had never planned on marrying anyone. He'd begun thinking of himself as a lone wolf. The idea of turning into the old bachelor sheriff had somehow taken root. He'd had visions of ending up like his father and having a girlfriend or two stashed away—ladies he could visit on Saturday nights. But in general the single life suited him just fine.

Now that Macy was hedging, Jericho felt ashamed to admit that her change of heart would seem like a reprieve. His only sorrow if they didn't marry would be T.J. But maybe things around the county would settle down enough now for him to spend more time with the boy despite not being his stepfather.

"Sheriff Yates." Dr. O'Neal met him just inside the front door. "I'd like to speak to you in private before you see the patient. Let's sit out here in the empty waiting room."

Jericho followed the doc. "What's wrong? Did the bullet do serious internal damage?"

Dr. O'Neal sat down on the flimsy, fake leather couch and removed his glasses. "No. Her gunshot wound is superficial. The bullet went right through the flesh on her left side and completely missed her ribcage. She twisted her ankle when she fell, but it's not broken or sprained. She also has some old bruising and a few nontreated cuts that appear to be at least twenty-four hours old. All things considered, her physical condition is unofficially 'beat-up' but not serious.

"That's not the worst of it, though," Doc added thoughtfully.

Jericho leaned against the edge of Doc's desk. "What are you trying to say?"

"She can't tell me how she got the bruises or the cuts. In fact, she doesn't remember a thing before this morning. I'm no expert in head trauma, mind you. But even with the small bump on her head, I don't believe she's suffered any major jarring of the brain. Certainly there's not enough outward damage to suspect a physical blow caused her amnesia.

"There *is* a condition known as a *fugue* state or psychogenic amnesia," he continued. "It's caused by a traumatic event so frightening to the patient that they flee from reality and hide themselves in another, safer life—one with no memories. I don't have a lot of training in psychology, but I do remember learning that this kind of state may last for months or years."

"Amnesia? But it's just temporary. The memories will eventually come back, right?"

"Hard to say," Doc hedged as he blew dust from his glasses. "I understand that in some cases snippets of memories will flash through the mind and memories may fade in and out until the full picture emerges. Sometimes…nothing comes back at all."

Jericho took a breath. He couldn't imagine how hard that would be. To never be able to bring back the memory of growing up or the memory of his mother's face. What would that do to…?

He jerked and straightened his shoulders. Whatever would possess him to think such a thing? His mother had been a drunk and had left the family when he was only a kid. Truth be told, he hated her. Why would he care to remember what her face looked like? That was one memory he wouldn't mind losing for good.

"Let's go talk to the patient, Doc. What's her name?"

Dr. O'Neal shrugged. "No clue. She doesn't remember and your deputy said he couldn't find any ID in her clothes or at the church scene."

Now, that was *one* thing Jericho would hate to forget. The Yates name meant something. There were generations of Yates men who had been lawmen, sportsmen and land-owners. It was a name to be proud of and to do right by.

Sheriff Yates. He'd worked hard to get that title. He'd paid his dues as deputy, been appointed when the old sheriff retired, and finally had been elected on his own merit. He anticipated continuing to be a man worthy of everyone's respect. And it was high time to do his job.

As Jericho walked through Dr. O'Neal's office door to meet the mystery woman, he didn't know what he expected to find. But it was definitely not the most gorgeous woman he had ever beheld.

Yet there she sat on one of Doc's plastic chairs. Miss America, Miss Universe and Venus de Milo all wrapped into one—with a bad haircut and wild, sky-blue eyes. Jericho had to swallow hard in order to find his voice.

"Good evening, ma'am. I'm Sheriff Jericho Yates. How're you feeling?"

She lightly touched her temple, but continued to stare up at him, those strange electric eyes boring holes straight into his. "The headache and the four stitches in my side are the worst of it. No, I take that back. Not knowing my own name is the worst of it. Did Dr. O'Neal tell you that I can't remember anything? He says I have amnesia."

"Yes, ma'am. I understand. But we need to talk about what you *do* remember. Can you start with your first clear memory and tell me everything that happened up until the time when you were shot?"

"Um…I guess I could do that." She reached up and rubbed the back of her neck. "But can you sit down first? I'm getting stiff just looking up at you. How tall are you anyway?"

Jericho found a chair and dragged it over while Doc moved to sit behind his desk. "Six-three." They both sat. "There you go, Red. Is that better?"

"Yes, thanks." Lost and feeling vulnerable, even in the presence of someone as safe as the sheriff, the woman had to take deep breaths in order to calm herself down.

"Did you just call her 'Red,' Sheriff?" The doctor was scowling over his desk pad.

The sheriff looked perplexed. "Well, I suppose. We've got to call her something. 'Hey you' just won't do and she has all that bright red hair. Seemed to work."

"Bright red hair? Do I?" She put her hands in her hair. "But that doesn't feel right."

"Don't upset yourself by trying to force the memories of your lost past," the doctor said soothingly. "Not yet. Give it some time." He turned back to address the sheriff. "Jericho, I want you to take things slow. Pushing her to remember will only make it worse.

"Oh, and I don't believe 'Red' is the least bit feminine," the doctor continued. "It doesn't fit this beautiful young woman and it doesn't sound respectful to me. Can't we come up with something else?"

Still with her hands in her hair, she worried that more

seemed wrong with it than just the wrong hair color. Though God only knew what she meant by that.

"Okay, Doc," the sheriff conceded. "How about 'Rosie?' That's in the same color type."

"Rosie's okay with me," she agreed quickly. The name didn't nauseate her nearly as much as the wrong feeling about her hair.

"Okay, Rosie," the sheriff said with a deliberate drawl and a tight smile. "You can call me Jericho. Now tell me what you do remember."

She wasn't sure she could do this. Every time she thought of how terrifying those men had been, her whole body started trembling. Looking up at Sheriff Jericho for support, she was surprised to find an odd softness in his eyes as he waited for her to speak.

She'd thought he had looked so tough. Scary-tough, with all his hard angles and rough edges, when he'd first walked into Dr. O'Neal's office. Now, it seemed that at least his eyes held some empathy toward her, and the idea made her relax a little.

"The…um…first thing I remember clearly is two men pushing me around. One was pointing a gun at me while the other kept shaking me by the shoulders, hard. I felt as though I'd just woken up from a deep sleep. But now I'm not sure that was the case."

"And these two men didn't look familiar?"

"Not at all."

"Where was this? What do you remember of your surroundings?"

"After a few minutes, I decided it had to be a cheap motel room. But I…never found out whose."

"Okay," the sheriff said as he rubbed a thumb across his neat mustache. "Don't strain for answers. Let's just take this nice and easy."

She must've been wearing a frown as she'd tried to bring the images to the front of her mind because that tender look had returned to Jericho's eyes. "Can you tell me what the men said to you?" he asked gently.

"Oh, yeah. They wanted to know where some special thing was." At his curious expression, she shrugged her shoulders. "I never found out what the 'thing' was they were looking for. But they said I had stolen it and their boss wanted it back."

"You believe what they were saying was the truth? Like perhaps you had stolen something?"

Yeah, God help her, it kinda did. But with that strange thought, she began shuddering again. A lone tear leaked from the corner of her eye. "I don't know."

"Sheriff…" The doctor cautioned him with his tone.

Jericho scowled briefly then nodded. "Sorry, Doc. I won't push.

"Okay, Rosie, what did the men say or do after you couldn't give them what they wanted?"

She sniffed once and wiped her hand across her face. "They beat me up a little. You know, like slapping me and punching me in the arms and shoulders. And the whole time they kept demanding that I talk. I was so scared they were going to kill me that what they were doing hardly even hurt."

The doctor cleared his throat. The sheriff fisted his hands on his knees.

"What did they say then?" Jericho asked in a rough voice.

"Finally, they looked at their watches and said I was going to go with them to see the boss. That he would make me tell where it was. Then they pushed me outside and into the backseat of their car."

"Did anything outside look familiar?"

Dr. O'Neal huffed and opened his mouth to chastise the sheriff's choice of words.

"Oh, yeah. Sorry again," Jericho put in quickly. "What I meant was, what did it look like outside the motel room?"

"I couldn't see much. But what I did see wasn't anything special. Like the poor side of lots of small towns, I guess." Now how would she know that? She couldn't even come up with her own name and yet she knew what the poor side of town would look like?

The sheriff gave her an odd look. "Do you know where you are now?"

"Your deputy told me. Esperanza, Texas."

"Does that hold any meaning for you?" Jericho glanced over at the doctor and then held up his hand in self-defense. "Don't answer that, Rosie, not unless something comes to you. I shouldn't have asked."

Jericho was more than a little frustrated. He didn't want to hurt her by asking the wrong questions. But the only way he could help her was by getting answers. He promised to think longer before he opened his mouth.

"Okay. Let's get back to the men. Can you describe them?"

"I guess so."

But while Jericho watched her open her mouth to try, he noted her wincing as another one of those slashing pains must've struck her in the head. "Never mind. Give it a rest for tonight. We'll try it in the morning. In fact, if you're feeling well enough by then, you can go through mug shots."

Rosie sighed and her shoulders slumped. She glanced up at him from under long, thick lashes with a look so needful, so vulnerable, that it was all he could do not to sweep her up in his arms and keep her bogeymen at bay. He'd never before acted as some female's sole link to the world and to safety. He was just a county sheriff. But whatever had frightened her badly enough to erase her memories needed to be dealt with soon. He vowed to be the one to take care of it.

"Jericho," Doc interrupted his thoughts. "Rosie needs a good night's sleep. We've determined that she doesn't have a concussion, but we haven't got any place to make her comfortable here. What can you do for her?"

"Leave this place?" Rosie folded her arms over her very generous chest in a self-protective move that stirred his own protective instincts even further.

There were no motels in Esperanza. The nearest one was a half hour away. It was too late to call anyone in town to find her a place for the night.

"But what if those goons come looking for me again?" Rosie's voice was shaky and her eyes wild and frightened again. "Will they? Do you think it's possible?"

Hell. It actually was a possibility that those men might double back and finish what they'd started. Rosie needed to be in protective custody. But where could he be sure she would be safe and comfortable? The deputy's substation in town had only a small holding cell. That would never do.

"Don't you worry, ma'am. You're coming home with me. You'll be perfectly safe and comfortable there. I've got a spare bedroom and it's all made up." Had he really just said that? He stood up and stretched his legs.

"Your spare room should be okay, Jericho," Doc said. "But there's something I must tell you both first.

"I haven't said anything to Rosie about this yet," the doctor continued. "Because I don't know if it might spark a memory and cause her some pain. But both of you need to know that there should be *someone* who cares about her and should've missed her by now."

Rosie sat forward in her chair. "What do you mean?"

"While I was examining you, I discovered you're around two months' pregnant." The doc said it carefully, gently, but there was no way to make that news go down easy.

"No." She put a hand to her belly. "Can't be. How could I forget something like that?"

The doc went over to put his arm around her shoulders. "It's possible that you didn't realize you were pregnant before you lost your memory. Two months isn't very far along. If you don't start getting your memories or haven't found a family by the time you're feeling a little stronger, come on in and see me for prenatal instructions.

"And in the meantime, watch your diet. No caffeine. No alcohol, and definitely no smoking. My examination tells me you've never carried a baby to full term before, but I'm sure you won't have any trouble. There are just some things you'll need to know."

"Yeah," Rosie said. "Like who I am and who the baby's father is." She shot Jericho a rolled-eye smile.

It was such an intimate gesture. As though the two of them already shared some gigantic secret from the rest of the world. In that split second, her smile miraculously swept away one of the invisible shackles to his normal restraint.

He could almost hear the snap of an old, half-forgotten anguish relinquishing its hold on him.

With a competent smile, he offered her a helping hand at the elbow. "Let's go. All of this will look better in the morning."

She stood and he did something he hadn't done in so long he could barely remember the last time. As they walked out of the doctor's office, he pulled her closer and they walked arm in arm together toward the truck.

Chapter 3

The moment Rosie stepped into Jericho's huge log-cabin home it seemed clear she'd made a mistake. Oh, the place was beautiful, with its handcrafted furnishings, sleek open spaces and heavy-beamed ceilings.

After taking a few steps past the wide front door, she spied a state-of-the-art kitchen, including dark granite countertops and stainless-steel appliances, that appeared prominently just beyond the stone fireplace.

Decorated in tans, browns and natural woods, the place certainly looked comfortable. And since Jericho was sheriff, it should be safe.

But where were the feminine touches? The walls held few decorations, save for a large fish mounted on a brass plaque and a couple of birds, or maybe they were ducks, stuffed and stuck on wooden planks. A bronze statue standing on a hand-hewed coffee table was the only other decoration she saw. Even the kitchen seemed stark and empty. This was definitely a man's home. A single man.

"Uh," she began. "Aren't you married? Where's your wife?" Why hadn't she thought to ask that before she agreed to stay here?

"I'm not married." He walked to the grand, airy kitchen and opened the refrigerator. "You want something to eat or drink? There isn't much. I was, ah, supposed to be on my honeymoon tonight."

She relaxed a bit. At least he had a girlfriend. "What happened? What stopped the honeymoon?"

He turned from the open fridge. "There was a shooting right outside the church. The wedding was called off."

"Ouch." She winced and slid onto one of the barstools at the counter. "I screwed it up, didn't I? I'm so sorry."

Leaving the refrigerator door standing open, Jericho crossed the kitchen and leaned over the counter in her direction. He laid a hand on her shoulder and the electric jolt his warmth caused against her skin both shocked and surprised her.

"Don't be too hard on yourself," he said. "Seems the bride-to-be was about to call the whole thing off. Temporarily, anyway. I'd bet she might even be grateful that you gave her the perfect excuse." He took his hand away and stared at it, as if he too had felt the sizzle.

With his hand gone from her shoulder, Rosie decided she could almost breathe again. "You don't sound very upset. Are you heartbroken?"

Turning his back, Jericho cleared his throat and went to the open fridge. "Naw. It was going to be one of those whata-you-call-'ems? Marriages of convenience. Macy Ward has been my best friend since we were kids. I volunteered to marry her and take over being the father to her out-of-control teenage son."

He glanced around the kitchen and then back into the nearly empty refrigerator as though he had never seen them before. "But I'm not sure where I figured we would make a home together. This place isn't set up for a wife and kid. I built it with my own hands, me and my dad, and I certainly don't want to move out of it and go to town.

"I guess I hadn't really thought the whole thing through well enough."

Maybe it was because of her jumbled state of mind, but she was having trouble processing everything he'd said. "You mean you two don't love each other but you were going to get married anyway? I didn't know things like that really happened." She shook her head. "Just so you could be a father to her son? Wow."

What was that she'd been spouting? How would she know anything at all, let alone about marriage? Was she married? She didn't feel like she was. Damn. The harder she thought, the hazier everything became. She must be more disoriented than she'd thought.

"Yeah, I guess that's about right." Jericho shrugged a shoulder. "You want tomato soup? I've got a can or two I can heat up and soda crackers to go with it."

Was this guy for real? "Sure. Soup will be fine." Maybe the whole thing was some terrible dream she'd been having. Any moment now she would wake up and find herself back to being…

Nope. The best she could do was to remember she'd been running for her life and had fallen at the feet of one deadly gorgeous, *single* Texas sheriff.

And tonight she would have to adjust herself to a whole new persona. Mother-to-be. Without so much as a smattering of memory of her own mother.

Not to mention, without having the first clue as to who the baby's father might be.

Hmm. All that might be more than she could handle for one night. Maybe she'd be better off doing what the doctor said and just go with the flow. At least for tonight.

So far she'd learned this Sheriff Jericho guy might be too good to be true. Marrying the best friend he didn't love in order to give her son a father? Good for him. And by the same token, that ought to mean she wouldn't have to worry about him forcing her to do anything against her will. Mister Knight in Shining Armor must be the ultimate good guy. Who woulda thunk a man like that really existed?

Rosie tried to let her mind go blank as she watched Jericho fumble around in the kitchen. But she couldn't get the idea of him being unattached out of her head.

As she looked down at her left hand, it made her chuckle to think that she would know about married women wearing wedding rings on the third finger of their left hands but she didn't know whether or not she was married herself. Her fingers bore no rings at all. But that didn't tell the whole story. What if she'd taken off her rings? What if they'd been stolen?

Sighing in frustration, she went back to studying the man.

Then wished she hadn't.

Wide, muscular shoulders flexed as he reached for dishes in the cabinets. His dark blond hair and sexy hazel eyes made him as handsome as any movie star. Her glance moved down along his torso as it narrowed to lean hips. She forced herself to turn away from the sight of his fantastically tight butt. But she didn't completely lose sight of his long arms and even longer legs. The whole picture was developing into a hero, all lean and formidable. Like the sheriff in a white hat from an old-time movie.

The good guy. The *sexy* good guy.

He set a bowl of steaming soup in front of her and sat across the counter with his own. "This must be tough on you."

Heartfelt concern shone from those deep hazel eyes as he gazed intently in her direction. The more she watched them, the darker the irises became. Soon they were steel gray, and suddenly sensual. Hot.

She quickly took a sip of the soup and nearly burned her tongue. "Uh, yeah. It's hard not knowing where I came from or who I am. I wish I knew what those men were after."

Jericho lifted the spoon to his mouth and blew as he studied the beautiful woman across the counter. He was having trouble keeping his mind from wandering. Wandering off to things he would love to do to her, for her, with her.

Her stunning eyes had lost that wild, crazed look, so

he'd been studying the rest. The body seemed made for sex. At five-foot-ten or so, she wasn't quite his height. But she also wasn't a dainty little thing, one who might break if he didn't watch his step. Somewhat on the thin side, she looked like a model. But unlike the models he'd seen on magazines, her lean body just made those fantastic breasts seem all the more voluptuous. And those legs. Don't get him started on those long, shapely legs. Even encased in designer jeans, he could tell how they would look naked—wrapped around his waist and in the heat of passion.

The mere sight of a good-looking woman had never done things like this to his libido in the past. He couldn't imagine why she was so different. But the why didn't seem to matter all that much. She just was, and he had to find a way to stop thinking about her like that.

She was pregnant. No doubt she belonged to someone—somewhere.

"Is the soup okay?" he asked, trying to push aside the unwanted thoughts. "Is there anything else I can do for you before I settle you down for the night?"

Ah hell. Just the word *night* made him long for things he had no business even considering.

"Soup's fine." She took another sip and a bite of the crackers. "But I feel so...I don't know. Like I'm not grounded. Like I'm flying around in midair. It's probably because I can't recall my past and my family. And this baby thing... That really threw me.

"Maybe it would help if you told me something about your family," she went on to suggest. "Would you mind? I think just hearing that someone else can remember and knows who they are will give me hope that someday I'll get my memories back. Does that seem too nosy?"

He was good at questioning victims and criminals. And he'd forced himself to become a decent politician in order to get elected. But talking about his life to a complete stranger was totally out of his realm. He had a strong instinct to keep his mouth shut, but she looked so vulnerable, so needy.

"There's not much to tell." But he guessed he *could* give her a few basic facts. "I was born and raised right here in Esperanza. My dad is Buck Yates, and he was born right here in town, too. Dad spent years in the service and now he owns the farm-supply store in town. Of course around here, that means he sells mostly guns and tack, some deer blinds and a lot of game feeders."

Jericho let himself give her one of his polite, running-for-office smiles as he continued. "My older brother, Fisher, is a captain in the U.S. Army, just home on leave from his third tour of duty in the Middle East." He shrugged and ducked his head, not knowing where to go from here. "That's about it for the family. Want to hear about my friends?"

"You didn't mention your mother. Has she passed away?"

If only she had simply died. "Our mother took off when Fisher and I were kids."

"Took off?"

"Disappeared. Haven't heard a word from her in nearly thirty years. She might be dead by now for all I know." Good riddance if she was.

He stood, picked up his empty soup bowl and eyed

Rosie's almost empty one. "You want another bowl of soup? Or anything else?"

Without answering, Rosie glanced up at him and he spotted dark, purplish circles under her eyes. The lady was whooped. His protective instincts kicked right back in again.

"Let's get you into bed for now. We'll have a fresh start in the morning. Okay with you?"

"I am tired. Thanks." She slid off the barstool and he watched her hanging tightly on to the counter as if her legs were about to give out on her.

He dumped the dishes into the sink and went to her side. "Here, take my arm. I won't let you fall."

For a moment, it seemed that she would refuse. Jericho saw her try to straighten up and steady herself. But within a split second, she started to slide.

There was no choice. He bent to pick her up in his arms. A lot lighter than he'd imagined, her body hugged his chest as she threw her arms around his neck and hung on.

"I feel ridiculous. I can't even remember my own name and now I can't walk under my own steam. It's a good thing you're here, Sheriff."

Yeah, maybe. Or maybe this was going to turn into his worst nightmare.

Jericho carried her down the hall and into the spare room. Setting her down in the corner chair, he pulled back the covers from the double bed.

"This should be comfortable enough." He had to turn away from the sight of clean, fresh sheets just waiting for bodies to mess them up.

"It looks great," she told him. "But I wish I had a pair of clean pajamas. These clothes are getting gamy."

He stood there for a second, picturing her naked again. Finally, making a tremendous effort, he started thinking with his head instead of another part of his anatomy.

"How about I lend you one of my T-shirts? I've got one or two older ones that've turned soft from washing and I don't wear them anymore. Would that do?"

She nodded and gave him a weak smile.

When he brought a shirt back into the room and handed it to her, his sex-obsessed brain produced another thought. This one worried him.

"Are you going to need help getting undressed?"

"No, I'm feeling stronger, thanks. I think the food helped."

"Great. The bathroom is right across the hall. There are towels in the closet and an extra new toothbrush. Use whatever you need."

"Thanks again, Jericho. I'll be fine. See you in the morning."

Glad to know she would be okay for the night, Jericho eased out of her room and headed for his own. He probably wouldn't fare as well with his own night. The thought of Rosie lying in bed in the room right next to his would keep him tossing and turning.

Sighing, he shrugged off his by-now-filthy dress shirt and tried telling himself it would all be okay. He had a plan. He would just start thinking of her like he would a roommate.

Well, that plan didn't work out so well. Jericho dragged himself into the shower the next morning and turned the faucets on full cold. *Roommate, my foot.* When had a roommate ever kept him lying awake for half the night with daydreams of long, silky legs and ripe, sensitive breasts?

Irritated at himself, he swore to do better today. And it would serve him right if he was too tired and miserable all day long to concentrate.

After his shower, he stood before the mirror, preparing to shave. A couple of things were going to have to change today, he silently demanded of his image. He needed to get a line on Rosie's relatives. Somewhere people must be missing her. The sooner he found them and returned her to her previous life, the better off he would be. Let someone else protect her.

The second thing that needed to change was the way she dressed. She didn't have a change of clothes, and she needed to cover herself up real soon.

But the thought of how she dressed reminded him of something else. Another chore he must do, first thing. Maybe he could combine the two. Yeah, that should work.

Rosie opened her eyes when a dash of sunlight hit her eyelids and irritated her enough to wake up. She glanced over at the bright sunshine peeping through the wood-slatted miniblinds and wondered what time it was.

Rolling over, it hit her. A gigantic black void. The gaping abyss in her brain suddenly threatened to swallow her whole.

Gasping for air, as though someone had been choking her, and flailing her arms against a sea of nothingness and nausea, Rosie let her mind grab hold of the only thing it could. The one thing she saw clearly. The memory of Jericho Yates.

Immediately her heart rate slowed and warmth replaced the stone-cold numbness she'd felt when she awoke to find nothing familiar. Jericho had made one hell of an anchor last night. He'd tethered her to the earth with quiet concern and a sensual smile.

Fighting to remain in the moment and trying not to think either backward or forward, she sat at the edge of the bed and took stock. First was the physical. Her head wasn't pounding as it had been last night. The stitches in her side were barely noticeable. She rotated her ankle and found only an echo of the pain she'd experienced.

Okay, so she felt a little achy and sore, but she would live. Well, unless the bad guys came back.

Her second concern—and the real question— remained the same as before: How was she going to get her memories back? The doctor said not to push it. The moment she'd tried to find some thread of memory, panic had set in.

Taking another deep breath, she came to the conclusion that she had no choice. To keep from going stark raving mad, she had better just go along minute by minute. Living hour by hour and feeling her way.

Standing in the kitchen drinking coffee, Jericho heard Rosie opening the spare room door and going into the bathroom. The sudden jolt of anticipation at seeing her again competed with the practiced calm he had almost perfected during the hours since his shower.

But just then someone knocked on the front door.

Jericho figured Rosie's goons wouldn't have the guts to confront him in broad daylight, and they definitely wouldn't be knocking when they came to call. So this must be the person he was expecting.

He checked out the window and saw her car. Yes, it was his best friend. He wiped the smile off his face and went to let her in.

"Morning, Macy. Thanks for coming." He stood aside and allowed her to come in.

When she entered the room, everything felt easy, even somehow more homey. "Good morning, Jericho. I had every intention of talking to you this morning anyway. It's my pleasure if I can be of some help at the same time."

As a best friend, Macy Ward couldn't be beat. As a potential spouse…he would just as soon skip it.

"I wanted to say how sorry I am about the ceremony, Mace. You know I wouldn't have ducked out on it if I'd had any choice."

Macy went straight into the great room and dumped her armload of folded clothes on the nearest chair. "I know. You're a good man, Jericho Yates. That's one of the reasons I twisted your arm into agreeing to marry me."

"Now, Mace. You aren't holding a gun to my head. I volunteered to help you out with T.J."

"Yes, you did. And I love you for it." She turned and touched his arm. "You are really a good guy, my friend. Too good to get saddled with a wife who won't ever love you the way she should. I can't do it to you.

"I'm calling the wedding off permanently," she blurted. "You're off the hook for good."

Relief mixed with sadness and kicked him in the gut.

He didn't want to get married, but he would do anything to help Macy out in her time of need.

"What about T.J.? How are you going to take control of him now?" When she didn't answer, Jericho stepped up again. "Look, I can make some extra time for him this summer. Just as soon as I find a link to our mystery woman, my schedule should lighten up."

Macy smiled softly. "T.J. is a big part of the reason I'm canceling our wedding. You know he's in the middle of doing that community service project you arranged for him over at the state park this week. He's not pleased about having to make up for the toilet-paper and mailbox mangling incidents, but I hope he's learning his lesson and is staying out of trouble.

"And then earlier this week Jewel agreed to let T.J. work at the Hopechest Ranch for the rest of the summer." Macy's smile brightened. "The hard work should be good for him. But that means you don't have to worry about making time for him. He'll be plenty busy."

Several emotions flitted through Jericho at breakneck speed. Disappointment came first. Then another level of relief. Finally, a streak of annoyance came and went. Now he would have no excuse for not spending all his time with Rosie and working on her case.

"Do you think T.J. is going to be broken up about the change in marriage plans?" He hoped not. Deep down the kid was really good and Jericho hated to see him hurt.

Macy shook her head. "Don't worry about it. Actually, he's been pretty antsy over us getting married.

I imagine he'll be happy to hear his mother will continue being single."

Jericho didn't like the sound of that. "Is he still upset over my giving him community service? I only did it to keep him out of the juvenile system. I…"

"No, Jericho," she interrupted. "You did the best thing for him. You're not trying to be his friend. Me neither. It's our job as adults to do the right thing. I really believe T.J.'s biggest trouble with the wedding is Tim's memory. He saw you as Tim's friend for so long that he couldn't quite get past the changeover to having you take Tim's place."

"But I wasn't…I wouldn't."

Macy chuckled at his mumbling protests. "I know. And T.J. would've found that out if he'd had the chance.

"But calling it off is for the best," she continued. "For all of us. This way, you'll have the opportunity to find someone who you can…"

At that moment, Rosie cleared her throat to announce that she was interrupting. She still had on his old T-shirt but she'd slipped on her jeans underneath it and her hair was wet from the shower. The sight of her in the hallway simply set his veins on fire.

The difference between how he'd felt seeing Macy and how he felt right now seeing Rosie seemed extreme. And he didn't care for it one bit.

Chapter 4

"You must be the one Jericho's calling Rosie. I'm Macy Ward." The woman rushed over and reached out to capture her hands. "Jericho's old friend. It's gotta be terrible for you, not having any memories. I was so shocked when I heard. You poor thing."

Taken aback by such an effusive greeting, Rosie felt torn between laughing and running for her life. But there was just something about Macy Ward that made her want to smile.

Slinging her arm around Rosie's shoulder, Macy hugged her close. "I brought you some decaffeinated teas and a few things to wear, honey. Just to get you by for a day or two. I can't imagine not having a closet or even a purse to call your own.

"Oh, makeup," Macy added with a start. "Darn. I should've thought of that, too."

"Um. That's okay. I don't know if I wear any." With that thought, Rosie lifted the back of her hand to her mouth in an effort to hold off what might turn into a sob.

But she stopped in midair, struck by the wayward idea that she might be a nail biter. Checking, Rosie was relieved to find her nails seemed intact. And manicured and polished at that.

So she was a woman who took care of her appearance. Spent money and time on it. Not that anyone could judge by the way she looked this morning. One glance in the bathroom mirror after her shower, and Rosie had nearly fled screaming. In addition to the bruises and cuts, her disaster of a hairdo could not possibly be normal. Not only didn't it look like she'd spent any money or time on it, but it just didn't *feel* right.

Rosie nearly broke down again as she wondered how long it might take her to get a clear idea of what her hair was really supposed to look like. Would that ever happen? It was possible, she supposed, that the memory would never return. But thinking that way made her knees weak.

Macy turned back to Jericho, who had been standing there with his mouth gaping open. "Jericho, fix Rosie this tea and us some coffee, will you? Maybe you could even scramble Rosie a couple of eggs. You *do* have fresh eggs?"

Being called down by Macy seemed to shake Jericho out of his reverie. "I've got a few eggs, and the coffee's already made. What are you going to do?"

"I'm going to help Rosie change. The things I brought should be a close fit to her size. She's a little taller and thinner than I am, though. So we'll have to see." With that, Macy spun them both around and headed down the hall.

Rosie heard Jericho mumbling from over her shoulder. "Well, sure. Y'all help just yourselves. I'll cook."

Fifteen minutes later and she was still feeling a bit weepy. Macy had been trying to brush her awful hair into some semblance of a style. Of course, without much luck.

Rosie thought things in general seemed a lot better. Macy bringing clean underwear had been a real blessing. Putting clean clothes on made Rosie feel almost human again. They'd discovered Macy's slacks were about an inch too short and the shoulders of her blouse were big enough for a Rosie and a half—yet the buttons in front barely closed. Still, clean clothes had made a world of difference in how Rosie saw her situation.

"I'm sorry I messed up your wedding yesterday, Macy. Are you upset? Can you reschedule?"

The other woman turned and captured her in a big bear hug. "You're a sweetheart for thinking of me when you have so much trouble of your own. But not to worry. The wedding is off for good. You didn't mess up a thing."

Rosie's curiosity was piqued and she decided she didn't care about sounding too nosy around this sweet woman with the blazing white smile and two tiny dimples. "Why did you call it off? Did something happen between you and Jericho?"

"Come sit down with me for a moment," Macy said as she led her back into the spare bedroom and plopped on the bed. "Let me tell you something about the man who's taken you in."

Curious, Rosie eased down beside her. She didn't remember a thing about her past, but maybe it would be smart to know a whole lot more about her present.

"When I was born in this small town," Macy began, "there were several boys who lived on my block. I guess I was kind of a tomboy as a kid because two of those boys who were my age became my best friends. I never had much to do with the other little girls in town."

It was nice hearing Macy talk about her past. Somehow her story seemed to be grounding Rosie.

"One of those two best guy friends was always acting as my protector and big brother. Countless times he saved me from bullies and rescued me from runaway horses and from out of trees." Macy's dimples showed at the memories. "By the time I was twelve, though, it was the other one who'd captured my heart. I developed a huge crush on that one and it quickly turned to love. We married the minute we were old enough."

"Jericho was the big brother of the two." Rosie was sure Jericho hadn't been the lover.

"Of course. He's still doing it, too. My husband, Tim, died about six years ago and Jericho stepped in to make sure my son T.J. and I were okay. I'm not sure what we would've done without him."

"But Jericho's never been married?"

Macy's smile dimmed slightly. "No. But in my opinion, it's just that he's never found the right woman. Everyone who knows him loves and respects him. He could've had his pick of any woman in the county."

"But not you? You're sure?"

It was a sad smile that Macy wore by the time she answered. "I wish I felt differently. But no. I'm sure. Jericho and I are like brother and sister. We'll never get past that. I know he's relieved to be getting out of our marriage agreement. But he's still the best man in the entire county.

"Who else would've agreed to marry his best friend just so her son would have a father?" Macy shook her head sadly and patted Rosie's hand. "Enough about me. How are you feeling? You look a bit pale. Are you queasy? Let's go get you something to eat."

For a split second when Rosie appeared out of the bedroom wearing Macy's clothes, Jericho had been absolutely positive the image he saw was all wrong. This mystery woman did not belong in cotton slacks and long-sleeved, button-down shirts, of that he was sure. He envisioned her as being more into silks and fancy designer duds. But then when he blinked once, the lost woman with no past was back and it didn't matter what she wore, his heart went out to her.

As the three of them sat around his kitchen table and Rosie ate breakfast, Macy babbled on about the current happenings in her life. Jericho suspected she was doing it to make Rosie forget her predicament.

"My boss, Jewel Mayfair—you'll love her when you meet her, Rosie. Well, anyway, she's had a kind of rough life. But her uncle is Joe Colton. He's that senator in California who's running for president, you know?"

Jericho cut in, "Macy, Doc O'Neal said we shouldn't

expect Rosie to bring back memories just yet. She's supposed to relax and just let things come to her on their own."

"Oh, but…" Rosie interrupted. "The name Joe Colton does ring a bell. He must be really famous."

"Or maybe you were just interested in politics." Macy added her own conjecture. "I know that the presidential campaign has been really heating up on TV. Jewel says her uncle has lots of influential backers. But since our Texas governor entered the race against Senator Colton, Jewel says things haven't been going so well. And I can imagine that's right. Governor Daniels is really hot. I voted for him for governor, and he can probably count on my vote for president, too. But don't tell Jewel."

Rosie chuckled, but then put her head in her hands. "I don't know. Everything sounds familiar but nothing is. The harder I try…"

Jericho would've liked nothing better than to take Rosie in his arms to comfort her just then. But Macy leaned over and lifted a gentle hand to Rosie's shoulder.

"Then don't try, sweetie." She turned to Jericho. "Maybe you could help Rosie by finding out the kinds of things she likes to do when she's relaxing. For instance, you know I love to read romance novels. I'm positive that wouldn't change about me even if I couldn't remember anything else."

Okay, Jericho had always figured he made a pretty good detective when it came to catching criminals. But this kind of detective work seemed a little over his head.

"Uh, what kinds of things would you suggest she try?" he asked Macy.

Macy raised her eyebrows and then tilted her head to study Rosie. "Most women would love a good relaxing day at a spa—along with some chocolate. But there aren't any spas around here. And I always love a good relaxing day of shopping, which is also in limited supply in Esperanza, Texas, I'm afraid.

"Um…" Macy looked around the great room as though something might come to her. "Maybe she has a hobby. Like sewing or knitting. Or…" She swung her arm around to indicate Rosie should look at the room. "Decorating. Does anything about this room speak to you?"

Rosie blinked a couple of times and then glanced over Jericho's furnishings. "It just says *man's man* to me," she said with a shrug. "Except I guess for the Frederic Remington bronze on the table over there, and that antique Navajo rug on the wall behind the leather couch that I suspect is worth several thousands. Those aren't museum-quality pieces, by any means, but they're nice examples of the style."

Jericho knew his mouth was hanging open. And judging by Macy's silence, she too had been surprised by Rosie's sudden show of knowledge. He'd almost forgotten he'd even bought the Remington at a charity auction. And the Navajo blanket had been a housewarming present from his father that he barely noticed anymore. Those were the only two things in the whole house except for his rifles that were worth much. Rosie had spotted them right away.

He finally got his voice back when Rosie turned to him. "Hmm," he said for lack of anything more definitive. "I suspect you've been either an art collector or a museum volunteer at some point in your life, ma'am. What do you think?"

"I don't know," she said with a heavy sigh. "I don't seem to know anything. I can't explain why those things just popped out of my mouth."

Macy stood and bent over Rosie to cuddle her around the shoulders. "Jericho, this poor girl needs to relax and not think too hard so her past can ease back to her. You've got to find something to help her."

He stood, too. "My job is to keep her safe and alive first, Mace. I'm worried that whoever tried to kill her will come back around for another try. We're just going to have to let the memories come as they will and see how she does."

An hour after Macy left, Rosie's head was still buzzing with Jericho's words. *Those men might come back for another try? Oh, God.*

"You awake?" Jericho poked his head inside the spare room where she'd been trying to take a nap.

Just the sight of him made her stomach muscles flutter.

"Yes," she said as she sat up at the edge of the bed.

"I've been on the phone with my deputy. And he's gathering some mug shots off the Internet for you to look at later today. You willing to give it a try?"

"Of course I am. I want those men caught." Thinking of those awful goons made her body shiver in dread.

"Easy there." Jericho took her hand and helped her stand. "I've also been giving some thought to hobbies that might make you relax. You still don't have a clue as to what you like, do you?"

"No." But having said that, Rosie's mind tricked her into thinking about one way to relax she wouldn't mind trying at all. Sharing a relaxing kiss—with the man whose soft hazel eyes were gazing into hers right now.

On second thought, Rosie admitted that kissing Jericho might not be as relaxing as all that. Just standing next to him now was shooting jazzy little sparks of lust right down her spine. Kissing him was bound to become more intense than relaxing.

How could Macy have turned him away? He was so hot.

"When I want to relax," Jericho began in his fantastic Texas drawl, "I always find being outside with nature is a great way to shuck your stress. Does that sound like something you might want to try?"

She shrugged, not able to concentrate on anything much more than a pair of to-die-for hazel eyes that were turning a gorgeous shade of sea-mist green that matched his shirt.

"What did you have in mind to do outside?" she asked. But in the next moment she wished she'd kept her mouth shut. She sure knew what she'd like to be doing—either outside or in.

"Well, usually I fish or hunt," he answered as though he had no clue what was on her mind. "Both real relaxing. But I suspect those might be too tricky for someone without memories. And it would take us too long to get out to the right spots for them, too.

"I was thinking, though," he added. "That you might be willing to take in some fresh air at the same time as I gave you a small lesson in self-defense. I have a target set up behind the house in the woods so I can practice with my service weapons when I need to. Think I can talk you into trying a little target practice? Maybe you'll find that relaxing."

"Self-defense?" Oh, Lordy. Just the idea made her anything but relaxed. "Do you really imagine that I might need to know how to shoot a gun?" Her stress quotient jumped at least a hundred percent.

Jericho grinned at her. "What makes you think you don't already know how?"

"I…don't… Maybe you're right. I should try lots of things before I just say no automatically.

"But do you truly think shooting somebody might be necessary?" she added warily.

"Slow down." He took her hand and slid his arm around her waist. "We'll go nice and easy. Just give target practice a try. Probably never going to need a weapon for any reason, but I'd just as soon you were comfortable around them all the same.

"Besides," he added with another grin. "I want you to meet my two hounds. I've been keeping them outside in their dog run for your benefit. But I know they'd like meeting you. Maybe you're a dog lover. You might even find out you've always liked target practice. Some people find it totally relaxing."

"Damn it all to hell, Arn." The hired goon called Petey swore again and spit out the window of their idling car, almost hitting a willow tree. "Unless she's dead, we can't go back without the chick. We'll be the ones in dead trouble. So what're we going to do?"

"The boss just now told me on the cell that he's sure she ain't dead, stupid." Arnie pocketed his cell phone and ran a sweaty hand through his hair. "No body looking like hers has showed up in no morgues. She's not even been booked into any hospitals round here. The boss can find out that kind of stuff."

"Crap! Can we skip then? Maybe get lost in Mexico?"

"Listen, you idiot, don't you know the boss has contacts in Mexico? He has contacts where you wouldn't even believe. There's no place you can hide from him. Just calm down and let me think."

"So where could she go?" Petey wasn't calm and he couldn't seem to keep quiet. "I know I plugged her at least once. I'm not that bad a shot, and I swear to God I saw her go down. There was a bunch of people around the church. Too many for her to crawl off into some hole to die."

"Shut up a second." Arnie rubbed a hand across his face and tried to think.

In a few seconds, Arnie was trying out his thoughts aloud. "Okay, so we know there was some kind of smoky at the traffic jam. He maybe made the tags. But we dumped them right away, so no sweat there. No chance in hell he got a decent look at our faces, either. I figure we're golden on that score, too. We're still just a couple regular dudes with nothing to hide.

"But the chick…" Arnie screwed up his mouth to think harder. "Somebody helped her. Took her in. Probably the smoky, or maybe some kind of doctor do-gooder in that crowd."

Petey started to whine, "But if somebody's helping her, she'll turn us in. Turn in the boss, too."

Arnie nearly cracked his imbecile of a partner across the mouth. "Weren't you paying attention, idiot? She said she couldn't remember nothing."

Petey shrugged. "I figured she was lying. Trying to save her skin."

"Yeah? Well, what if she wasn't? What if some sucker is helping her and she can't tell them nothing?"

"Then we're in the clear. Let's get out of here."

Huffing in frustration, Arnie rolled his eyes. "We've gotta find her. The boss ain't gonna give up just 'cause she's lost her mind. I'm guaranteeing you, we don't bring her back, and we're dead meat. Finished. You understand?"

Petey nodded his head but couldn't get a word out of his trembling lips.

"Fine," Arnie said almost absently. "So we're gonna go see what we can find out about her. Somebody will know something in a town as small as Esperanza, Texas."

"How? Who's gonna tell a couple of strangers anything?"

"Shut up, Petey. I'm doing the thinking. In every small town there's a couple of places where people know stuff and don't mind spreading it around. If you was a woman, we could go to the beauty parlor. You find out all the gossip in them places."

Petey opened his mouth as if to complain, but Arnie threw him a sharp look.

"I saw just the right place for us back down the road a ways," Arnie said. "You know, I think you and me are in need of new hats. I've been meaning to get me one of those cowboy hats, anyway. Pulling the brim down over my eyes will make a perfect disguise. And I'm thinking you'd look pretty decent in a John Deere cap."

"Aw, crap, Arn. I don't like caps. Can't I get the cowboy hat? Where are we going get this stuff anyway?"

Arnie put the sedan in gear and pulled out of the roadside park. "Do me a favor, idiot. Do not say one frigging word while we're in the store. Not one, you hear?"

"Yeah. Yeah. But where?"

"Where every old codger in town usually shows up every day," Arnie told him with no small pride in his voice. "And all of them cowpokes can't wait to spill their guts around so they don't have to go back to work too fast."

At Petey's frustrated look, he gave it up. "At the farm-supply store, of course."

Chapter 5

"Is this the correct way to hold it?" Rosie asked as she grasped the weapon with both hands and pointed it at the target. "It doesn't feel right."

Jericho scraped both his sweaty palms down his pants legs and tried to figure out how he'd managed to get himself into this fix. It was one thing wanting the woman to be able to defend herself and quite another completing the mechanics of the thing without touching her.

He'd been standing a minimum of six feet behind her, spouting instructions at the back of her head. Now he lowered his eyes to take in her slender back, narrowing to the tiny waist. A little lower and his gaze stuttered across her small but firm butt encased in Macy's old jeans. Then his wayward eyes strayed further to look their foolish fill as his stare wavered on down those long, sexy legs. Holy mercy, but those long legs could sure give a man dreams he ought not have.

His attraction to her could not be tolerated or indulged. Too close, and he was bound to give in. She was too tempting, with her sexy body and her vulnerable but bright eyes. He knew with his whole being that if they ever made love, he might find he wanted to keep her forever. Or some other such nonsense in the same vein.

Jericho had a good life here. His father lived and worked nearby and they talked nearly every day as family should. He'd grown up with all the people of this town. People like Macy and Tim, Clay and Tamara Brown and Clay's brother, Ryder, and his sister, Mercy. Some of them were gone now, either dead or moved away. But still Jericho's roots here were strong. He didn't need anything else in his life.

The people of this town and county knew and respected him. Depended on him. That was where his energies should be focused. Not on a pair of lost, sky-blue eyes.

Okay, so maybe on some particularly lonely nights, being single in a small town wasn't all he'd ever wished for. It could be stark and depressing. That was a fact.

"Jericho?" Rosie turned to see why he hadn't answered. "Is this right?"

Tamping down his hormones, Jericho stepped up to the task. He slid in close to the warmth of her back and wrapped his arms around her in order to show her the correct stance by example.

The zing of electricity between their bodies almost knocked him back again. But the sheriff of Campo County had to be stronger than all that.

"Not exactly," he murmured into her ear. "Here, I'll put my hands on top of yours to show you the right way. Just relax."

The minute the words were out of his mouth, he knew they were both in trouble. Each of them took a deep breath, straightened up and cleared their throats.

Rosie's body trembled against his chest, but he felt he had to finish what they'd started. After a few more minutes, he couldn't have said how he'd ever managed to stand his ground and show her the correct way of pulling the trigger while keeping her eyes open and aiming at the same time. But, he had, and she'd hit the target—twice. So he backed off and took back his weapon.

"You seem to be a natural at shooting," he told her as he clicked on the safety. "But to tell the truth, you don't seem very familiar with guns. How does it feel being outside?"

"Weird. Like maybe I don't get out in the sunshine too often. But I kind of enjoy it." She stared into the woods behind the tree where he'd set up the target. "I'm not crazy about the wild though. Isn't it kind of scary in the woods? I don't think I'd care to go in there."

Jericho chuckled and took her elbow. "Okay, then. We'll cross hunting and fishing off our list of possible ways to relax." He headed them back toward the house. "Let's go to town and see if Deputy Rawlins has some photos for you to look at."

Rosie smiled at Jericho's deputy as he shook her hand. At just about six feet tall, Adam Rawlins seemed to be in great physical shape. But even with all his muscles, the deputy still didn't appear as formidable as the sheriff.

"We'll catch those bastards," Adam told her with a polite smile. "Don't you worry, miss."

She walked with Adam toward a computer that was stored in an alcove at back of the sheriff's office. Meanwhile, Jericho went to one of the two large desks in a different section of the large room. Even just a few yards away, Rosie felt bereft without him by her side.

Adam pulled two folding chairs up in front of the computer and motioned for her to have a seat in one of them while he sat down beside her. "Let me show you how to work this. It's pretty easy."

The deputy smiled over at her and she knew he'd intended to put her at ease. But his perfect brown hair with every strand in place and his sympathetic brown eyes that were studying her carefully didn't come close at all to settling her nerves. His hair wasn't the same dark blond color as Jericho's and didn't occasionally go astray due to having strong hands stab through it with frustration. Not like Jericho's. And the plain brown eyes of Deputy Adam weren't at all the same as Jericho's hazel eyes that could change from gray to green—all depending on the weather and what the man was wearing that day. Nothing about the deputy sitting next to her did a thing for her nerves.

Trying to hide a secret sigh, Rosie returned her attention to the computer. "Yes, I think I've got it," she told Adam. "The program doesn't look all that complicated. You don't have to sit with me. I'll call you if I run into trouble or if I spot anyone who looks familiar."

"Yes, ma'am." The deputy gave her a half smile as he stood and walked toward his own desk.

Rosie shot a quiet glance in the direction of the tall man wearing a long-sleeved white shirt and uniform tie standing across the room and bending over a desk loaded with paperwork. In contrast to sitting beside the deputy, just the sight of Jericho sent her pulse racing and her stomach bouncing. Whenever Jericho touched her, little firecrackers exploded inside her chest. Her palms grew damp, and her thighs trembled. Learning to fire a gun at the target this morning beside him had been a trial of fighting lustful thoughts and urges.

Things were so unsettled in her mind. But one thing stood out clearly. She wanted that man to want her. Badly.

"Is she all right over there by herself?" Jericho asked his deputy.

Taking a quick look in the direction of his boss's gaze, Adam nodded his head. "Yep. Frankly, I think the lady's better at using that computer than I am. Seemed to pick up on it right away."

"Yeah? Well, that should tell us something about her. I just wish I knew what it was besides the fact she knows computers."

Adam threw his boss a hesitant smile. "Yes, sir. Do you have any ideas regarding how we should go about starting our investigation? Where we should begin if she doesn't spot anybody from those mug shots?"

Jericho released a breath and turned away from the sight of Rosie's long legs bunched up under her as she sat at the desk. He rubbed absently at the back of his neck.

"Start with missing persons. Check all the wires to see if someone of her description is listed.

"She's a real looker, don't you think, Adam?"

The deputy nodded. "Except for the hair, I do."

Jericho frowned at Adam's truthfulness, but then shrugged it off, believing the choppy cut and unnatural color only added to her appeal. "So someone in this county or nearby must've seen her at least once before she ended up shot at the church's doorstep. She didn't just appear in the back of a car in Esperanza out of thin air.

"Why don't you start asking around?" he suggested. "Check the gas stations and the truck stops. And go on over to my dad's feed and supply store. Everybody in the county shows up there sometime or other during the day. Find out if any of the ranchers spotted her or one of those goons driving through or stopping to ask directions."

"You bet, boss. I'll go right now. You can help the woman with the computer if she finds anyone familiar, can't you?"

Yeah, Jericho thought. He could help her. And he would, damn it. Nothing else mattered quite as much to him at the moment.

Frustrated and tired, Rosie clung to Jericho's arm as they strolled down Main Street and prepared to cross at the corner, heading toward Miss Sue's town café. It seemed as if over the last couple of hours she'd stared into the faces of hundreds of men, all terrifying and snarling at her from the computer monitor. But none of them had been the ones who'd hurt and kidnapped her.

Worse, being outside in the fresh air now after

studying all those criminal faces was giving her the creeps. Every man who either drove by or walked in her general direction made the hairs on her arms stand straight up. Some kind of internal instinct must be calling out, demanding that she run and hide. Stay out of sight.

Definitely someone somewhere wanted an unknown thing from her badly enough to send goons after her. She was positive they wouldn't give up so easily.

"You okay?" Jericho asked as she took a couple of deep breaths. "Still want to grab a bite at Miss Sue's? You wouldn't want to miss her pecan pie."

"Um…yes. I guess so." Rosie looked up into Jericho's face and found a concerned expression, half hidden by the brim of his uniform's cowboy hat. "It's just that I can almost feel someone watching me. Waiting for me."

Jericho stopped directly in front of the café's door. "I take gut feelings seriously, ma'am. So I can't say for sure it's not possible that those guys are in town and waiting. But I guarantee you they won't be inside the café. And I promise I'll be guarding your back when we leave.

"All right with you?" he asked. "We have to eat sometime, and while we're here I can check with some of the folks about your case. What do you say?"

She threw a quick glance over her shoulder and saw nothing but an ordinary small-town street and loads of bright sunshine. "I say, I'm with you, Sheriff. Lead on."

Jericho did just that. He walked them inside, and hesitated long enough to flip his hat on a peg next to the door. He then found an empty table in the center of the room, away from the huge curtained windows that looked out on Main Street. Rosie could've kissed him for being so thoughtful. In fact, she could've kissed him just for being so broad-shouldered and steely-eyed. And, actually, she intended to find a time to test his kisses as soon as she could get him alone.

The tough but friendly sheriff greeted every person in the café with a smile and a personal word. Rosie guessed he must know them well since he'd lived here all his life. But no one looked the least familiar to her.

The café itself seemed old but spotless and well cared for. Homey. The mismatched wooden tables and chairs were all full of smiling, happy people who seemed to be enjoying their food. Shouldn't a place as comfortable as this feel as though she'd been here before? She'd wanted it to be familiar. But it wasn't.

Jericho ordered for them, since she hadn't a clue what she might like to eat. Within minutes their lunches were delivered.

"Why do I have a salad?"

"Well now, that's easy. I've found that pretty, thin ladies like you seem to go for salads at lunchtime. Does something else sound more appealing? If so, Becky will be happy to fix you anything you want."

Without warning, her eyes filled with tears.

Swiping at them, she tried to explain. "I hate this. I hate not even being aware of what I like to eat. I hate looking into people's eyes and not knowing if I've ever met them before." She gritted her teeth and fought back the sob threatening in her throat.

He put his hand over hers on the table and squeezed. "It's hard, I know. But the doc said for you to take it slow. Pushing could make things worse."

"Forgive me, but the doctor doesn't have goons hiding nearby in the shadows who want to kill him," she said with a whine in her voice she didn't care to hear but couldn't seem to help. "None of you can know how hard this is."

"True," Jericho said with another light squeeze of her hand. "But most of the people in town will be happy to watch out for you once they learn about your problem. Give them a chance."

Somehow certain she had never been able to depend on anyone the way Jericho was saying she should depend on the whole town, Rosie heaved a heavy sigh. "I'll try."

"Good. And in the meantime, why don't you give the taco salad a chance, too. You might be surprised."

That made her smile. And relax a little. At least, she relaxed enough to discover that the taco salad tasted pretty good. And that she'd been really hungry.

Just as they were contemplating ordering the pecan pie, a nicely dressed woman with short golden-brown hair stepped into the café and looked around. Her warm eyes skipped over every table as though she were searching for someplace to sit. The sight of someone like that who looked a little lost, got to Rosie. She immediately thought of this woman as a kindred spirit.

When Jericho spotted her, he stood and issued an invitation for the woman to join them at their table. Instead of being frightened, Rosie warmed to the thought of getting to know the lady with kind eyes and a friendly smile.

"Rosie," Jericho began after the woman had been seated with them and they'd all ordered pie, coffee and a glass of milk for Rosie. "This is Jewel Mayfair. She's Macy's friend and her boss at the Hopechest Ranch."

He tilted his head toward the woman he'd introduced as Jewel. "This here's our mystery lady, Jewel. I've been calling her Rosie because we don't know her real name."

Jewel extended her hand across the table. "Hi, Rosie. I've heard about you and what happened yesterday from Macy. I was certainly sorry to hear about your troubles. Are you feeling okay now?"

"I'm okay. It's just…frustrating…not knowing anything."

"I'll bet. But I'm sure it will all come back."

As she'd said those words, Jewel's expression had turned melancholy. She looked so depressed and forlorn suddenly that Rosie couldn't help but reach out.

"Are you all right?" Rosie stared into the other woman's face for a moment and discovered deep circles under her eyes. "Aren't you feeling okay?"

"Oh, yes," Jewel told her quietly. "I just haven't been sleeping well lately. That's all."

"Is there something wrong out at the ranch?" Jericho asked. He turned to Rosie. "Jewel runs a new state-of-the-art facility designed specifically to help troubled teens. She tries to give them a stable home base and good hard outdoor work while they're in treatment. I think it's a great idea. Been needed in these parts for a long time."

Returning his attention to Jewel, he said, "There's nothing wrong with any of the kids, is there? Or anything I can do to help?"

Just then the waitress brought out their plates of pie and drinks.

Jewel emptied a sweetener packet into her coffee mug and took a breath before she answered. "It's nothing, Jericho. Just my same old nightmares finally getting the better of me, I guess."

"Nightmares?" Rosie hadn't thought about dreams. Would she have any? Would they be scary or about the good times from her past that she couldn't remember in the bright light of day? "Are they horrible? What do you dream about?"

Jewel looked startled by the question. Rosie could scarcely believe she'd asked such a nosy, none-of-her-business type of thing.

"Sorry. I shouldn't have asked."

Turning to Jewel, Jericho gently put a hand on her shoulder. A dart of jealousy flew into Rosie's chest before she could block it. Such silliness. What was wrong with her? She'd only known Jericho for about twenty-four hours. She simply could not have any feelings for him this fast. And besides, she'd been wanting to take Jewel's hand for support herself.

"You don't have to talk about this, Jewel," Jericho told her. "It's too personal."

So Jericho knew about Jewel's past. Maybe that was just normal for a small-town sheriff. Or maybe they shared something special between them.

"No, it's okay." Jewel tilted her head back to Rosie. "I'm a psychologist. We believe that the more you talk out your demons, the less hold they'll have over you. So I don't mind you asking.

"It's all ancient history, anyway," Jewel continued. "Not something I should be afraid about now. But I still have these nightmares that I…"

"I think I'd rather not remember the bad stuff," Rosie blurted.

Jewel actually lifted the edges of her lips in a half smile. "Sometimes I wish I could have a little amnesia—just about this one thing from my past. But unfortunately, it was a too-real car accident. When I close my eyes, it still seems as clear to me today as it did when it happened a couple of years ago."

"I'm so sorry," Rosie wished she could drop into a hole and cover her head. She didn't want to hear the details. "Were you injured?" she asked anyway.

The other woman sighed. "Yes. And hospitalized for a long time. But that wasn't the worst of it. My fiancé had been driving us out on a date in my car that night. He was killed instantly—along with our unborn child. I…"

Rosie couldn't stand to hear any more. She leaned forward in her seat and whispered, "But you're a psychologist. Isn't there something you can take to make you sleep without the nightmares?"

"No, there's nothing you can take for nightmares," Jewel told her with a note of familiarity that indicated she felt a bond to Rosie. "I've gotten in the habit of taking strolls around the ranch when I can't sleep. It's nice out—usually. The stillness of the night. The vastness of the stars in the heavens. The stock softly baying in their pens. Something about it soothes me. If you have bad dreams, you might try walking."

"Absolutely not." Jericho had been quietly listening

to their conversation, but now he broke in. "And you need to stop going out alone after dark, too, Jewel."

"Oh, Jericho…" Jewel began, skepticism showing in her voice.

"Listen to me," he interrupted. "Remember, it wasn't that long ago a body was found on Clay Colton's ranch land—in a spot right adjacent to the Hopechest. And you—"

He turned to Rosie. "Just yesterday someone shot at you in front of a ton of people at the church. I'd rather you didn't walk anywhere alone. If you need to walk, then let me know. I'll be there to watch your back."

Chapter 6

Rosie's eyes went wide, but then she ducked her head and quietly sipped her milk.

Okay, so maybe he'd come on a little strong. But the idea of anything else happening to Rosie had gotten him all riled up.

Jewel sat, looking down and ringing the edge of her cup with a finger. "I've invited my teenage half brother, Joe Colton, Jr., to come visit for a couple of weeks. I'm hoping the company will help, if that makes you feel any better, Jericho."

An awkward silence spread over the table and Jericho decided he'd be better off to step away from it. He looked around the room and spotted a couple of county road workers that he might be able to question.

"You two be okay here?" he asked, but without expecting an answer. "I'll take care of the bill. Y'all sit as long as you like. I'll just be right over there."

As he strode across the room, Jericho thought he heard the two women whispering behind his back. But he was glad Jewel had befriended Rosie. Jewel's California sophistication seemed a better match to whatever Rosie had been in her past than his rural upbringing would ever be.

He was still trying to puzzle the mystery woman out. She wasn't an outdoors girl, that's for sure. Though, she had definitely taken to the dogs. Both old Shep and the collie puppy Chet nearly loved her to death when she'd stopped to pet them on the way to target practice this morning. He'd been left standing to the side, wishing he could've joined in the fun.

Whatever relationship was developing between him and Rosie had become a primal pull that he was having difficulty ignoring. But giving in to it just wasn't like him. He'd always been a right-is-right kind of man.

After a few minutes of questioning the two county road workers as they ate their lunches and finding himself getting nowhere, Jericho was relieved to hear his name being called out. He turned to find the deputy coming his way.

"Glad I caught up to you, Sheriff." Adam looked calm and cool, even though he'd just come in from the heat of the day. "I wanted to give you an update."

Jericho thanked the road crew and found an empty table so he and the deputy could talk more privately. "Any of the missing persons reports seem promising?" he asked.

The deputy shook his head. "Sorry, boss. I went back through the files for the last six months but didn't come up with anyone who even looked close to our mystery woman's description."

The waitress brought them glasses of water, but they declined anything else. "All right. That's fine, Adam. We'll keep checking around. When you get back to the office, why don't you put out a bulletin to the neighboring counties concerning Rosie and her situation. Something should turn up shortly.

"What else did you get done on Rosie's case today?" Jericho asked.

"I went on over to the feed-and-supply store like you said," the deputy answered as he picked up his water glass. "By the way, your dad says to say 'hey.'"

Jericho nodded, imagining his father's Texas drawl and the casual way he always held his body to make sure everyone felt at home.

"And your brother Fisher asked about the wedding," the deputy added. "I guess he's staying with your father while he's in town, right? Anyway, he wanted to know if the ceremony has been rescheduled. Told him it wasn't any of my business."

Chuckling to himself, Jericho could just imagine Fisher's attitude with the deputy. "If anyone asks you again, Adam, you can say the bride has called the wedding off."

"Yes, sir." The deputy sipped his water. "I left word with your father to check with everyone who comes in the store to see if they can remember anything about the woman or that car.

"But I'm thinking now I'd better get back to the office," Adam added. "On my way home later I'll swing by the truck stop and check with a few of the drivers. See if anyone remembers seeing a woman with crazy red hair."

"Fine. Good work. Something is bound to turn up eventually. Maybe by tomorrow."

Jericho wasn't exactly thrilled about having Rosie stay at his house for another night. Either Jewel or Macy probably would've taken her into their homes for a few days—and maybe he should've asked them for the help. But he'd rather not take the chance of putting anyone else in jeopardy. Someone was still after Rosie. He could feel it in his gut.

Having the mystery woman stay with the sheriff ought to keep her safe. No one would be crazy enough to attack her while she was with him.

Rosie sat back in her chair at the table as she listened to Jewel and Becky French, the café's owner, discussing the first stages of a pregnancy. Maybe she ought to be more attentive to their discussion since she'd been the one to start the conversation by asking questions. But she couldn't muster a whiff of interest in the subject.

In her mid-sixties, Becky was short and plump and seemed like the perfect embodiment of a grandmother. In fact, the first thing the woman had done when she sat down in Jericho's place was to drag out pictures of her own grandchildren in order to show them off.

Something felt familiar about Becky. Rosie stared at her over the rim of her milk glass, willing herself to remember. But whatever had caused that spark of recognition in the first place blew away like a smoke trail in a strong wind.

Did she have her own grandmother somewhere who looked like this one?

Whenever a wisp of a half-remembered memory strayed just out of her reach, she immediately thought about not having anyone. The feeling of being all alone in the world overwhelmed her again and again with paralyzing fear.

What kind of person had she been? Did she have a big family? Lots of brothers and sisters, friends and neighbors? She could only hope that she'd at least been a good person. All that talk from those goons about her having stolen something was worrisome. Was she a thief?

She supposed that if she'd been dishonest the police would have some record on her. Perhaps the deputy had come up with something already. It was a scary idea, but at least then she would know who and what she was.

Looking toward the table where Jericho and his deputy were temporarily seated, Rosie wondered what they'd found out so far. If she was some kind of criminal, she wanted to know for sure. Even if that meant having to face justice somewhere.

She watched Jericho closely. Every single person she'd seen interacting with him so far seemed to have the ultimate regard for the man.

What she wouldn't give to have people think of her in that same way. Was it possible she'd been like that in her previous life?

Maybe she would never remember who she had been

before. Maybe they would never be able to put a name to her face. Then she could build an entirely new life. Starting from today.

If things went that way, Rosie wanted her new life to be like Jericho's. She vowed to make every moment count from now on.

Jericho and Adam rose from their places and walked toward her table. As he came closer, Jericho looked so strong and dependable. It made her want to curl up in his lap and let him protect her from everything. From everybody.

She wanted him. Wanted him to be her sheriff and protector. Wanted him to help her build a new life and become her family. She just plain wanted him.

"Everything good over here, ladies?" Jericho grinned and straddled an empty chair to sit down. "Maybe we should be on our way if you're done."

"Y'all stay as long as you want," Becky told him with a friendly smile.

"Well, that's very nice of you," Jewel said. "But I have to get back to work."

Jericho turned to speak with Becky while Adam took Jewel's elbow and walked with her toward the restaurant's front door. Rosie was left sitting there. She got up and eased toward the door herself so she could bid Jewel goodbye, too.

"I was wondering if you might be willing to join me for supper this Friday night?" Rosie could hear Adam talking quietly to her new friend and she slowed her steps to give them a little privacy.

She couldn't hear Jewel's response, but the other

woman was smiling sadly and shaking her head. Looked like Jewel must be turning the deputy down.

In the next second, Jewel turned and glanced longingly back at Rosie. She seemed to be asking for help.

Rosie walked over beside the other two. "I didn't get a chance to say goodbye, Jewel. Wait up."

Adam nodded his head at the interruption, excused himself and turned away to join the sheriff. Jewel hustled Rosie out the front door of the café so they could say goodbye and not be heard.

"Are you going out with him?" Rosie whispered.

"I can't. I know it's been almost two years since my fiancé died, and Adam seems like a nice enough guy. But I'm just not ready."

Rosie felt terrible for her new friend. "You need to start living again, Jewel. Look at my circumstances. If I don't find out who I am, I'm going to have to build an entire new life. And I won't be able to do it by hiding my head—even if that's what I'd rather do.

"If I can do it, so can you." Suddenly, Rosie's eyes welled with tears and she was forced to flick them away with the back of her hand.

Jewel took her other hand and squeezed. "You're such a dear person. But I suspect you're a lot stronger inside than I am. For me, it's just too soon."

Rosie felt ridiculous being so weepy all the time. Had she always been like that? She straightened up.

"I don't know why I'm so emotional," she told her new friend. "It doesn't seem like I was that kind of person before. But how can I know for sure?"

Jewel patted her shoulder. "Maybe it's because

you're pregnant. Anyway, that's how I felt during my first few months, too. I cried at every little thing. Then after the accident…. Well, I can't possibly have any tears left at this point. I must've cried an entire ocean."

Rosie wanted to hug her friend, but her instinct told her to back off for now. "Maybe you're right to be cautious about dating," she hedged.

She should give herself the same advice. But with Jericho… Well, it was just different with him somehow. She felt like they'd known each other forever. And when it came down to reality, perhaps it would eventually turn out that her *forever* had started yesterday.

"I'd better go check and find out if Jericho wants to go," she said quickly to change the subject. "Will I see you later?"

"I'm really busy at the ranch right now. But maybe Jericho can bring you out to see our operation and meet the kids sometime."

Rosie hoped so. This life might not be her real life, but she was feeling more and more comfortable here and in her new skin.

She said goodbye to Jewel and then returned to the café—only to find Jericho and Adam donning their hats and getting ready to leave themselves. Jericho was still busy saying goodbye to Becky.

But the deputy turned to her and then slid a glance over her shoulder. "Did Jewel go already?"

The tint of a blush rode up Adam's neck. Rosie thought the idea of the tough deputy having a crush on Jewel was sweet.

"Jewel said she had to go back to work, Adam." The

man's crushed expression made her feel bad and urged her to keep on talking, hoping to take the sting out of his rejection. "Did you find out anything about my past so far?"

The deputy shook his head sadly and took her by the hand. "Sorry, ma'am. Nothing yet."

Not as much a surprise as a wake-up call, she found that Adam's hand in hers lacked the same energy as Jericho's. There was no zing with the deputy. No sizzle.

"I wish there was something I could do to help," she said. Then she thought of those goons' scary words about stealing and quickly decided it was time for her to push the issue, even if it meant learning an unfortunate truth. "Have you checked to see if I'm wanted by the police somewhere?"

The deputy reared his head back slightly, narrowed his eyes and dropped her hand. "No, ma'am. Should we?"

She opened her mouth to say yes when suddenly Jericho stepped in close and answered for her. "We've been operating under the assumption that she's the victim, deputy. And I still believe that'll turn out to be the case. But maybe we should cover all the bases. Rosie and I will come back to the office on our way out to my cabin and let you take her prints and a mug shot. Then run them through the Texas system and also through AFIS."

Jericho's eyes were dark and bright as he watched her closely. He looked dangerous as hell. Rosie really hoped she wasn't on the other side of the law from this man. He was probably deadly against his enemies. And she would much rather remain his friend.

The deputy nodded curtly and went on his way.

Jericho took a deep, cleansing breath. He was trying

his best to get his inappropriate jealousy under control. When he'd turned and found Adam's hand on Rosie, his temperature had flared. But feeling this possessive of a mystery woman was just insane. What if she turned out to be a criminal and was faking the amnesia?

No, his gut told him that wasn't right. She couldn't possibly be anything but a victim. Her eyes said that much.

"Come on," he told her.

As he took her elbow, electricity ripped through his hand. His fingertips burned with the mere touch of her skin. He felt more alive and dynamic standing next to this woman than he had in longer than he could ever remember.

"Let's go back to the station and get this over with," he said gruffly. "Then I think we'll stop out by my dad's store on the way back to the cabin. Okay by you?"

She nodded and slipped a hand into his. The sparks exploded between them again. Every time he touched her, no matter how casually, he felt as though he had been branded. He wanted desperately to make her his own. To brand her in return so that everyone would know to keep their hands off.

Unfortunately, the ideas of what he *should* do and what he *must* do were beginning to merge in his mind. Right and wrong had always been clear before. Now all he could visualize was the gray lying in between the black and white. Lust was making him think in ways he'd never done before.

Stupid. Stupid. Stupid.

The handsome and powerful man excused himself from the lavish party and slipped outside to the terrace.

As he went, a dozen beautiful women watched him walk by with lust plainly apparent in their eyes. Too bad he couldn't take them up on their unspoken offers. He had too much to lose right now to give it all up just because he couldn't keep his fly zipped. No matter how tempting.

Checking his cell messages, he found the one from his hired man, Arnie, he'd been expecting. It was about time. After listening for a few moments, he lit an after-dinner cigar and returned the call.

"But, boss." Arnie was hedging with a whine clear in his voice after being chastised for not completing his mission. "She's staying with the sheriff himself. We don't dare try to take her as long as she's with him."

"I said to make your move *now*. Before things get any further out of control. And I expect you to follow orders. I want that woman here within a few hours."

"But boss…he's the sheriff."

"How many men does he have guarding her?"

"Just the sheriff."

The boss *tsked* aloud and chewed on his cigar. He never had trouble controlling his irritation. That's how he had gotten this far. But now he felt a pang of pure anger beginning to crawl up his spine. It made him weak. Unacceptable.

He blew out a breath and vowed to keep his cool this time, too. "Then do as I say. A small county sheriff in Texas is nothing to me. He won't cause you any trouble. Do whatever you need to with him. I can fix it later.

"But I want her back here by tomorrow," he added. "Or else. And no excuses this time. Do you understand me?"

Chapter 7

Rosie waited in the back of the farm-supply store with Jericho's father, while Jericho joked around and told stories with his brother. The two over-six-footers were standing in an aisle near the front windows. Afternoon sun hung low in an orange sky and flowed through the windows, bathing both men in a warm glow as they spoke quietly together.

No customers were in the store at this hour. Just the three Yates men—and her.

Jericho's father made her feel comfortable. Like she almost belonged here. She didn't mind waiting for Jericho and getting to know his father at all. At six feet tall himself, Mr. Yates was still in great physical shape. He wore his gray-streaked hair cut close to his head, and his tanned, leathered skin spoke of a lifetime of outdoor living.

"You sure have two fine-looking sons, Mr. Yates."

"Call me Buck, please. Everyone does." The older man shot a quick glance at his two boys and then turned to study her. "I always tried to raise them with strong values of patriotism and service, and that much seems to have taken hold. But raising good-looking, community-minded men hasn't helped me a bit in getting grandchildren. I had hopes that Jericho might be on the right track with Macy, but…"

"Oh." Did Jericho's father blame her for getting in the way of their wedding? "Maybe it was all my fault that the wedding didn't happen. But Macy said…"

"Hold on there." Buck interrupted her with a grin. "I know those two weren't really meant for each other. Not over the long haul. As a matter of fact, my son never once in his life looked at Macy the way he looks at you. It's a good thing he didn't ruin two lives by marrying the wrong person before the right one came along. I did that myself and have regretted it ever since."

"The way he looks at me? He doesn't even know who I am for sure. What do you mean?" She pulled herself up a little straighter and held her breath. It had always seemed to her that Jericho's eyes were questioning her, so Buck's answer seemed all-important. But she wasn't entirely positive why.

Buck patted her shoulder. "He looks at you as if he could eat you in one gulp. As if the sun had never shone on the world until you showed up. It don't matter how long two people know each other. That kind of feeling only comes along once in a lifetime. And my son's got it for you."

Did Jericho feel the same things for her that she'd been feeling for him? How could something like that happen so soon? And in the middle of such terrible confusion and terror.

"I…uh…" Buck started to speak, but his expression had changed from pleasant and hopeful to wary and sad. "That is…I didn't do my sons any favors by not remarrying after their mother left us. I was so sure I could be both mother and father to them that I didn't believe we needed anyone else.

"Trouble with thinking that way, though, is that Jericho was too young at the time to do without a mother." Buck shook his head and frowned. "He never understood why she'd left and never quite forgave his mother for not coming back. I'm sure he blamed himself, but that couldn't be further from the truth. I think he must still have a lot of anger inside him that needs to come out before he can ever be really happy. That's why he's never found anyone before now."

Anger? But that certainly didn't sound like the Jericho Rosie was beginning to know. All right, so maybe he thought of himself as a dedicated bachelor. But was he single because he wanted to be or single because he didn't trust a woman not to hurt him?

Geez. Rosie suddenly decided she was thinking too much. Where had all these crazy amateur psychology ideas come from anyway? Was that what she had been in her real life? A psychologist?

No, that didn't sound right at all. But on the other hand, how could she know anything anymore? Her whole life before Esperanza, Texas was a big fat blank.

Just then, Jericho and Fisher came up the aisle toward them. "You ready to go back to my place?" Jericho asked her.

The warmth Jericho caused by standing so close flamed across her skin and made her wonder if going back to his house was such a good idea.

Yes, she suddenly decided, it was. Getting closer to him was all she wanted. There was nothing she needed more than to plaster herself as close to him as possible. Had Buck been right about Jericho's desire?

There were so many things Rosie couldn't know because her mind had blocked them. But Jericho's desire for her was one thing she had the power to discover in the here and now. And she vowed to force the issue if she had to.

Twilight had arrived. In the parking lot behind his father's store, Jericho unlocked his pickup and turned to help Rosie climb into the passenger seat. But when she stepped closer, he was hit by a blast of yearning so forceful it nearly knocked him to his knees. He wanted her. Badly. Yet he'd known that before. This time, though, it seemed like something more than lust.

As he took her arm, he tried to come up with why this need felt different. *Safe.* That was the only word he could think of to define what he was feeling. He'd been trying so hard to keep her safe that it never occurred to him she might be the one to make him long for security. But as he looked into her eyes, it was like nothing he'd ever experienced before.

Family. For the first time in his life, someone besides

his father and brother made him yearn to be part of a family. This lost woman and her unborn child needed him in a way no one else had—including Macy and T.J. On more of a primitive, survival level.

"Jericho?" Her eyes searched his.

He'd been standing here staring for too long. Abruptly, he threw his arm around her waist to help her into the truck's cab. But he stumbled in his haste, and she reached for his shoulders to steady them both.

Inside, he was anything but steady.

Too close, their gazes locked as a sudden change came into her eyes. She fisted a hand in his shirt and dragged him even closer, though the whole time her eyes stayed intent upon his. Automatically, one of his hands went to her hair, stroking, soothing, until it finally eased its way down to cup the base of her neck.

Time hung between them, like the magic first star in the night sky that hovered just above the horizon. Then came another change. She murmured something low, clamped her hands on both sides of his head and dragged him down for a kiss. Many kisses.

She nibbled and nipped. Licked and sucked with such desperation that Jericho could barely keep up.

His mind went blank. Nothing was making any sense. Nothing but the surety that if he didn't return her kiss right now, this minute, he was going to die.

Giving in to his own desperation, he slanted his mouth over hers and kissed her as if it were the last thing he would ever do. But instead of the end of something, he wanted this kiss to be the first kiss she remembered. His kiss—not some dude's from the depths of her murky past.

As he returned Rosie's wild lust, he put his whole being into it. He ran his hands along her body, drinking in every curve. Soft. Yielding. Sensuous. Jericho absorbed the details, wanting to experience them all.

His hands burned as he touched her everywhere. His lips were set afire by her kisses.

"I want you, Jericho," she whispered against his mouth. "I feel alive with you. What's between us is right. I know you feel it too. Show me. Please."

The sounds of her urgent pleas knocked the sense back into his muddled brain. Thankfully, just in time. Another minute and they would've been sprawled together across the front seat of his pickup. And though it was getting darker by the minute, they were still in the brightly lit parking lot of his father's empty store.

Jericho gently took her by the shoulders and set her back from him. "This isn't right." He eased her up into his arms and slid her into the pickup's front seat.

Striding around the cab, he slipped behind the wheel and started it up. "You must belong to someone—somewhere. If we give in to our hormones tonight and tomorrow your memory comes back, along with a husband, you would never forgive yourself—or me. I won't take that chance."

"What? But…" Her voice trailed off as he put the truck in gear and pulled out of the lot. She folded her arms over her chest and stared out into the night.

Gritting his teeth, Jericho silently fought an internal struggle with fluctuating ideas of right and wrong. And he also battled to bring his overheated body back into line.

Frustrated as hell. He couldn't wait to get home and into a shower. A cold one.

The ride back to Jericho's cabin through the dark countryside was long and silent. Rosie stared out into the night, wishing Jericho would say something. Every now and then, the lights from someone's house shone in the distance. She took those opportunities to sneak a glance over at the man doing the driving.

He gripped the wheel with both hands, so tightly that even in the darkness she could see his knuckles turning white. He had wanted her. She didn't know very much of anything right now, but that had been clear when he kissed her.

Perhaps his father was right and Jericho did want her in a way he'd never wanted anyone before. That knowledge would help her because she couldn't even say the same for herself. She wanted him, all right—but had she wanted someone else the same way once before?

Damn, this was so frustrating. She began wringing her hands in her lap. Needing to think this romance thing through better, Rosie ticked off the few points in her favor as the black night flew by outside her window.

The two of them were attracted to each other. That was good. They seemed to have a definite chemistry. That was also very good. So what was stopping them?

Jericho had been about to be married when she'd fallen into his life. That could be bad. But then Macy and Jericho had both made it clear they didn't love each other and the wedding was off. Good for her again.

So now how about her own past? She was pregnant

with someone's child. And of course, that had put a serious damper on Jericho's desire a few minutes ago. But deep down Rosie didn't feel that there was anyone else, even though someone had obviously been with her—at least once. She'd thought and thought, scoured her feelings, but the only emotions she felt from the fog of her past were scary. Fear. Not love.

And if there had been someone, why hadn't he reported her missing? That was the number one unanswered question making her feel positive she was alone.

"Hell." Jericho took his foot off the accelerator and peered through the windshield down his own long asphalt driveway as the outside lights from his cabin burned through the darkness before them.

Rosie looked up, too. "What's the matter? Is something wrong?"

Jericho left the truck idling for a moment. "Everything looks fine. But…" He rolled down his window. "The dogs aren't barking. And there's just something—not right."

He put the pickup into neutral, flipped off the headlights, and reached around to eye his rifle, which was hanging in a rack in the back window. "I'm going to turn the pickup around, drive to the main highway and leave you there parked and locked in the truck. Meanwhile I'll call the deputy to come meet you while I hike back here to check things out."

He turned forward without unracking the rifle. Instead, he pulled his cell phone out of his pocket—just as a loud ping sound hit the truck's front bumper. Dropping the phone, Jericho rammed the truck into gear, hit the gas and spun in a one-eighty.

"Someone is shooting at us!" Rosie shouted above the noise of the engine revving.

"Right. Get down!" He flipped open her seat belt and shoved at her back.

She slid all the way to the floor and covered her head with her arms. Rolling into a tight ball, she squeezed her eyes shut and prayed.

Jericho cursed under his breath as he straightened the wheel and stomped on the accelerator again. He wished for the cell phone that was now out of reach on the floor somewhere. They needed help.

Hoping he could escape, he raced wildly down his own driveway. Good thing he knew every inch of this asphalt drive. He'd built it with his own hands.

But just when his pickup was within a hundred feet of the highway, moonlight picked up the shadow of a massive SUV pulling into the driveway from the road and blocking their exit.

Slamming on the brakes, Jericho came to a stop. Sweet mercy. They were surrounded.

Another series of blasts, sounding like they must be coming from an assault weapon of some sort, exploded through the air. The shots completely missed them, but Jericho didn't figure they'd be so lucky a third time.

"Yipes!" Rosie screeched from the safety of the floor.

How many were there? At least two. One in the SUV and one nearer to the house. Jericho was fairly sure they hadn't managed to break through his carefully constructed security and gotten into his home. But he needed to get inside there himself. Inside was a way to call for help and plenty of firepower to hold them off until help arrived.

Reaching over, he grabbed a handful of Rosie's shirt by the back of her collar. "Take your seat again and buckle up tight," he ordered.

"What are you planning?" she asked shakily as she rose to her knees.

Even though he didn't answer, when he jerked upward, she pushed herself back into a seated position. Then he waited one more second to make sure she had the safety belt tight enough.

"Hang on and stay low." Without considering other consequences, he swung the wheel to the right and pointed his truck off the driveway toward the empty fields. Then he hit the gas. The pickup jerked and roared ahead, breaking through a wooden fence he'd only just finished building last month.

Jericho plowed his truck through the rangy field. With the headlights still off, he prayed silently that none of the pickup's tires would hit a recently dug prairie-dog hole. Damned varmints never stopped digging, no matter how he had tried to stop them.

He and Rosie were lucky on this night. He heard the pickup's four-wheel drive cutting in as needed, and on a few occasions, the tires spun in the dirt before he slowed and allowed them to catch again. It didn't matter that they were bashing through prickly pear cactus and past tall, spindly wildflowers. His good ole truck made short work of it. He refused to think about what this wild ride might be doing to the paint on the sides and fenders. What was a new paint job when it came to saving Rosie's life?

At last they'd almost crossed the open field and reached the tree line beyond. There was only a half-moon tonight, but he wasn't having any trouble seeing where he was going. He knew it all by heart.

"Stop! Watch out for the woods," Rosie shouted from her seat next to him.

Apparently she wasn't having much trouble seeing in the moonlight, either. Jericho hoped to hell the bad guys' positions had been far enough away that they weren't seeing their escape route quite as well. And God help them if these goons had night-vision goggles.

He slowed the truck just a little at the tree line and drove right between two tall ebony trees. Hearing Rosie gasp, Jericho wished he had time enough to explain. But for his plan to work, he had to keep concentrating on his driving.

If the bad guys were smart enough to listen, they would certainly be able to hear the pickup's engine, even though the truck would be hidden by the woods. Because of that, he should turn the pickup off as soon as possible. But fortunately, he knew that people unfamiliar with rural areas would not think to step outside their vehicles and pay attention to the noise. He had to hope these perps were city boys.

Dodging through the sparse trees, Jericho judged their position and decided it must already be close to his destination. Sure enough, another few feet and he felt the front tires making contact with caliche. The ancient road through the woods that ran from an abandoned homesite—situated maybe a few hundred yards behind his cabin—to the main highway might be overrun with weeds and pockmarked by the weather. But it would take him where he wanted to go.

And where he wanted to go was not back to the highway. He was counting on that being what the bad guys would figure. That he would make a beeline for the highway, trying to escape. But Jericho knew the stretch of highway running in front of his acreage was always pretty deserted at this time of night. So he turned his truck in the other direction and headed toward the old homesite.

He spared a swift glance toward Rosie and saw her hanging on to the door with all her might. She was badly shaken by this bumpy ride. But at least she was alive.

As the pickup neared the relic of the ancient cabin, Jericho cut the engine and let it glide up to the clearing. When he thought they were in the best spot not to be seen through the woods, he parked and took the first breath he'd had since the original rifle shot had hit the truck.

"We're right behind my cabin—out a few yards behind those targets I set up." He shifted and drew his service weapon. "Here. This is similar to the gun you were using to practice this morning. I want you to keep it and stay with the truck." He handed the Glock over and then turned to bring down his rifle.

"You're not leaving me here." Even in the darkness he could see her trembling.

"You'll be safer here. I'm going to sneak up to the house and get in through a hidden basement door. I won't be able to move as fast or as quietly with you in tow. Stay here where I know you'll be safe."

"Why are you going to the cabin? Why aren't we running for our lives in the other direction?"

"Trust me," he said. "They won't be expecting me

to head right for them. This'll be the best way—a real surprise."

Hefting the rifle with one hand, he quietly eased open the door but flipped off the overhead light. Then he reached around under his seat with his free hand.

When he straightened, he held up something small. "Here's my cell phone." He shoved it at her. "Call 911 the minute I'm out of sight. Tell them Sheriff Yates needs help at his cabin. And also tell them you're waiting in my pickup by the old Gaston place. They'll come, but it may take twenty minutes."

Before he stepped out, Jericho shifted close and seared a quick kiss across her lips. "Please stay put. No matter what you hear. I'll come back for you as soon as I can."

She blinked a couple of times and then stared down at the weapon still fisted in her hand. "Okay," she answered in a shaky voice.

Rosie watched Jericho slide noiselessly out of the truck and shut the door behind him. Within seconds he disappeared into the darkness.

She called 911 and the operator also told her to stay where she was. After hanging up, she was all alone again.

Her heart thudded so loudly in her chest that she was afraid it would give her away. Her eyes had adjusted to the darkness, but every shadow seemed to move. The black night began closing in on her.

She couldn't just sit here. If one of those men happened to spot the truck, they'd have her captured in an instant. Not sure she could use the gun and sorry she had promised to stay put, Rosie made the decision to move. To hide in the trees, away from the pickup.

Easing out her door, she carefully shut it again. Then, putting the phone in her pocket and holding the gun with both hands, she tiptoed across the caliche and into the forest in the same direction as she'd last seen Jericho.

Shaking badly and with her back against the rough surface of a tree, she stopped to catch her breath and listened for any sounds. Nothing. No night noises of any kind. No car engines. No whispers or footsteps close enough that she could hear.

She closed her eyes and tried to calm down. But then it happened. A loud click sounded through the night. Close by. Had it come from over by the truck? Was it the sound of a weapon being prepared to fire? Or was it someone's footsteps breaking a twig beneath their shoes?

It didn't matter which one. She had to get away. Adrenaline shot through her veins, giving her false courage and agility as she stepped out and made her move.

Chapter 8

Rosie had been holding her breath for the last fifteen minutes. Hadn't she? Hiding behind the largest target Jericho had set up in his backyard, she exhaled and peered toward the back of his cabin through the spotty moonlight.

Suddenly staccato bursts, which she thought must be guns firing, echoed through the night. But they seemed a long way away. Were sounds deceiving out here? And who had been doing the shooting—and who may have been shot? The next moment brought total silence again.

Weren't there outside lights in the back as well as the front of the cabin? It seemed as though this morning she'd noticed a few tall posts at the edges of Jericho's backyard that she'd assumed were lights or electricity. Now there was nothing but darkness.

Curiosity got the better of her. She had to find out what was going on.

Creeping out from her hiding place, Rosie wondered if she would be too exposed even in the dark by cutting across Jericho's yard. She slipped the gun into her waistband and dropped to all fours. Crawling might cause her hands and knees some damage, but maybe she would live longer by keeping a lower profile.

After slithering a few feet, her hands were covered in nasty burrs from the sticker bushes. Another yard and her skin began to sting. Ants! Cripes.

Was it worth it to stay low? Someone from above must've been watching out for her, because right then she felt the raindrops start against her back and neck.

Rain would be a good cover, she thought. So she stood, dusted off the ants and stickers as best she could and moved on through the windy mists, hopefully still in the direction of the cabin.

Did she know how to pray? Had she been a churchgoer in her previous life? Rosie couldn't say, but still, she tried begging for mercy in the only way she could imagine.

Please, God. If I was a bad person, then don't help me now for myself. But keep me safe for Jericho's sake. She knew the sheriff well enough by now to know if he lost her, it would devastate him.

The rain began coming down in sheets then, and she gave thanks for the shield it provided. But in the next moment she found herself totally turned around. What direction was the cabin? Rosie could barely tell up from down.

Frozen in panic, she swiped the water out of her eyes

and tried to reason. Should she keep on going straight ahead? Had she turned her body at all after she'd stood up and the rain started?

A disturbing noise reached her ears through the sounds of rain splashing against the dirt. It sounded for all the world like someone moaning. Jericho?

Had he been injured? If so, he would need her help.

Sucking up all her courage, Rosie put her hands straight out in front of her body to run interference in case she smashed into any trees or walls. And then she took her first tentative steps, going in what seemed to be the same direction as the moaning sounds.

Shuffling along, she went quite a few yards, totally blinded by the rain. Then the weather eased up a bit, allowing her to see the dark shape of the cabin straight ahead. She stopped to listen.

There. The same unsettling moans. Closer to the cabin's back wall. She inched ahead again.

Nearby. She felt she was almost on top of the sounds now. Did she dare call out?

Dear Lord, what shall I do?

Out of nowhere a siren's scream pealed through the night. Help was coming! Thank heaven. They were saved.

"Jericho," she rasped in as loud a whisper as she dared. "Where are you?"

Another blind step and Rosie tripped over something large and inert, lying on the ground. She put her hands out in front of her body to take the brunt of her fall. But it wasn't any use.

Down she went. In the next instant, her nose buried itself in mud and muck. Ugh. As fast as possible, she pushed herself up and tried to roll over to catch her breath. The mud clung to her, sucked her back down.

Damn it. All she could think was had that inert object been Jericho's body? Rosie forced herself up to crawl backward. She had to find out.

Quickly losing his grip on self-control, Jericho slammed the door to his empty pickup, still sitting exactly where he'd left it, and cussed under his breath. Where the hell was she? She'd promised to stay here.

He knew the bad guys hadn't had a chance to kidnap her. He'd been keeping them plenty busy over the last half hour. First with the surprise of having to fight off his firepower. And then with trying to get away after they'd heard the sirens heading their way.

At least they hadn't gotten away totally clean. He'd winged one of them as the guy had been making a dash toward his buddy in the SUV. Jericho was sure of it. He was also positive their SUV had taken several hits as he'd fired at their retreating backside.

Both Deputy Rawlins and a deputy from another part of the county had arrived at the scene at the same time. The other deputy had taken off in pursuit, but Jericho didn't figure he would have much of a chance of catching the SUV that'd had a few minutes head start.

Now where the hell was Rosie?

"Lend me your cell, Adam," he said to his deputy.

"Sure thing, boss." Adam threw him a phone and then began edging around the clearing with his flashlight studying the ground.

"There won't be any decent prints left after that rainstorm," Jericho told him. "I'm going through the woods toward the rear of my cabin. You go on back to the house by way of the highway and see if you can spot Rosie anywhere along the road."

They split up and Adam retreated carefully down the ancient caliche road in the direction of the highway. Jericho flicked on his own flashlight and headed into the woods at approximately the same spot where he'd gone in an hour ago.

In a few minutes, he came out at the edge of his property line. Going left, he found the emergency shutoff for the outside lights and turned them back on. Earlier darkness had saved his ass. Now it was keeping him from finding Rosie. She had to be somewhere close.

He stood for a second, letting his eyes become accustomed to the floodlight. Then, thinking he heard a snuffling noise, Jericho moved closer to his cabin. In the direction of that noise. Pulling out his deputy's phone, he put it to his ear and punched in his own cell number.

It began to ring, but the ringing was much clearer in his free ear than in the ear next to the phone. His own phone had to be somewhere nearby.

"Hello?" He heard Rosie whispering into the phone.

"Where are you?" he demanded. "You were supposed to stay put."

"Jericho? I need you. I'm out behind…."

Her sentence was interrupted when Jericho's flashlight beam roamed across her face. "Here I am. Help me, please."

Through the beam of light, Jericho saw her sitting on the ground in half shadow just a few feet behind his cabin. She looked like someone had covered her in mud and weeds. Her tear-streaked face was caked and intense. If he wasn't mistaken, she also seemed to be holding his old shepherd's head in her lap.

"What the hell?" He bent on one knee. Sure enough, Shep's body lay perfectly still and Rosie was murmuring something quietly in the old dog's ear.

"I think he's still alive," she said. "But…but…"

"They poisoned him." Jericho's blood raged. He had to grit his teeth against the idea of anyone hurting his animals.

Thrusting the flashlight into Rosie's hand, he carefully scooped up the dog. "Lead the way toward the kitchen door. As soon as we get him inside, I'll call for help. Then I'll need to come back out and look for Chet."

At the mention of his name, the collie appeared out of the shadows. With his tail between his legs and shaking his head as though to clear it, the collie didn't look all that strong, either.

"Good boy, Chet. We've got your buddy now. Don't worry. Come inside."

Rosie opened the door, flipped on the kitchen overhead light and stood aside so he could bring both dogs across the threshold. Jericho took one look at her in the bright light, and his heart sank.

Not only hadn't he managed to keep his dogs safe, but the one person he'd been determined to save tonight looked like she'd been dragged through hell.

Nice night's work, Sheriff.

"Thanks, Quinn. I appreciate it." In the early hours of the morning, Jericho stood at his front door, saying goodbye to his neighbor, Quinn Logan, a large animal vet. "I know dogs aren't really your business, but I'm not sure mine would've made it without your help."

Rosie stood back a few feet and listened as Quinn prepared to leave. She ached all over. And even though she'd washed her face and hands, her body was still covered in mud. However, she was much more concerned for her host than for herself. He'd been so pale and quiet as they'd tried to make the dogs comfortable and waited for the vet.

At first, after they'd come into the dry, safe house, he'd been all business and strong as he'd dealt with the deputies and made phone calls about their attackers. Then a little later, when they were sitting on the floor with the dogs in the kitchen, she'd caught Jericho trembling while he stroked the coat of his old shepherd. She almost knew how he felt. If Shep died because someone was after her, she would never be able to live with herself.

"Well, I didn't do much," Quinn told Jericho. "I wish I could've done more for the shepherd. Your collie should be fine by tomorrow. But it may be touch and go with the older dog for a few days."

"What kind of poison do you think they used?"

Quinn, a man about Jericho's height but with an easygoing manner and sensitive eyes, shook his head and took a breath. "Not sure. But if I had to guess, I'd say it was probably an illegal human drug. Maybe something like PCP, which is easy to get on the street, and acts like an anesthetic in animals. As a powder, it would've been simple to add it to hamburger and feed it to the dogs.

"If it'd been anything like a real poison, the dogs wouldn't have lived for this long."

Jericho cleared his throat and looked down at his boots. "Yeah, well…"

Quinn clapped him on the shoulder with a gentle hand. "There's nothing else you can do but wait. Get some rest yourself."

The vet tilted his head in Rosie's direction. "I'm thinking the humans in this house need as much attention as the animals. Both of you look like a strong wind might blow you over."

Jericho shot her a quick glance. His eyes softened as they took in her messy appearance. Then he turned to finish telling the vet good-night.

After he locked the door and set the security alarms, Jericho took a few steps in her direction. He held his hands out, and Rosie thought he might take her into his arms. But something stopped him and he dropped his hands limply to his sides, shaking his head with hesitation.

"Why don't you take a shower and hit the sack?" he said as he brushed past her, heading for the kitchen. "You heard Quinn. I'm just going to check on the dogs once more then collapse myself."

"Aren't you worried about those men coming back?"

"Not tonight." Jericho's lips actually quirked up into the semblance of a smile as he stopped and turned. "I'd bet those goons are going to be busy finding a way of tending their wounds without going to a legit doctor who would be bound to turn them in. They won't even think of us again tonight. Then, for tomorrow night and every night until we come up with answers, I've already lined up a watch system. My brother, Fisher, and a couple of deputies from other parts of the county have already volunteered to stand guard in shifts. I'm sure a couple of our neighbors wouldn't mind helping out, either."

"Oh, no. That's too much trouble because of me. Maybe I should leave. Go…" *Where?* Where could she go?

Jericho's expression tensed as he shook his head. "You're safer here than anywhere else. Let us watch out for you while we figure out where you came from. None of the people around here mind taking up the cause of your safety. It's what we do in these parts. We watch out for each other."

Rosie brushed her fingers over her burning eyes. "Thank you, Sheriff. I suspect your friends and neighbors will help because of you, not me.

"But I don't seem to have a lot of choices, do I?"

He stood watching her intently for several moments without answering. "Go on to bed. We'll figure out something eventually. And in the meantime, just remember you're safe."

Turning his back then, Jericho headed into the kitchen to look after his animals. Miserable, but out of both choices and energy, Rosie forced one foot in front of the other and made her way toward the shower.

At the very least she could clean up. It was one of the only things she could do to help herself.

A half hour later, Jericho stood barefoot in front of his bedroom mirror, staring at his own image. Naked to the waist, he bent over the dresser and beat his fisted hands against the top. What a jerk he was.

Damn it! He'd been so scared when he'd thought he might've lost Rosie. It made him sick to his stomach to think of it.

Gulping in air, he wondered what the hell was the matter with him. She wasn't his to lose. She didn't belong to him. In fact, she clearly belonged to someone else.

His dogs were resting easy now. He couldn't worry too much about them for what was left of the night. But he had a feeling he wasn't going to be faring as well as they did, what with Rosie right next to him in the other bedroom.

After he took a couple more deep, calming breaths, an odd noise reached his ears. Someone seemed to be in trouble nearby.

He stepped out into the darkened hallway and stood still to listen. The noise was much clearer from this spot. What he'd been hearing with the door closed was definitely the sound of a woman's sobs. Coming from his bathroom.

He'd thought Rosie was already asleep in her room. Something must be wrong with her. But what should he do about it?

It sounded for all the world as if her heart were broken. But maybe she'd been hurt. What if she'd cut herself and really needed his help?

Hell.

In three big strides, he was at the bathroom door. He tried the knob, hoping to peek in and check on her without her noticing him. The door was unlocked, so he held his breath and opened it.

When he could see inside, he found the bathroom

awash in limited, flickering light. Just the two night-lights were burning, but the overheads had been left off.

Rosie stood in front of the bathroom mirror, looking at herself through the dim light in the mirror. And sobbing uncontrollably.

"You okay?" he whispered. "Do you need help?"

She gasped, and it was only then he noticed she didn't have on any clothes. She didn't turn around but grabbed a towel and held it to her body, trying to cover the intimate parts.

But she couldn't cover her long, lovely backside. And he let himself take it all in. From the crown of her strange red-colored head, down her slender neck and past the slim torso all the way to her perfectly rounded buttocks and those mile-long legs. My God. She was perfect. He'd known she would be. But this was better than all his idle dreams.

"Go away. I'm…okay," she began with a stutter. "No, that's not true, Jericho. I do need help. I need…"

She started to turn, but then their eyes met in the glass and she halted. She blinked and licked her upper lip. "The doctor said it was all right to shower, but not to get the bandage too wet. It seems I got the dressing all muddy earlier. So then I tried to change it myself, but I…can't reach."

Jericho watched as the tears began again. They glistened against her cheeks in the low light and swamped her beautiful blue eyes.

"Let me," he said and took a step closer.

Rosie tried to stem the flow of her tears. What an idiot she must be. It was a simple thing. Just changing her bandage after a shower. But when she couldn't seem to help herself, she'd remembered how all alone she was and the tears poured in earnest.

Jericho was being so nice. But nice wasn't really what she wanted from him. She wanted—well, she wasn't sure.

Glancing up into the mirror over the sink, their gazes met—and locked. Oh, yes. That's what she wanted from him. Whatever that was, there in his eyes. Was it a hunger? A wanting so desperate he looked ready to pounce.

"Give me the bandage and show me where," he demanded roughly.

Her heart pounded wildly as his gaze lowered to the edge of her towel in the mirror. She could feel her nipples tighten painfully in response to that look. She wanted him to touch her there, relieve her aching.

"The bandage is on the counter," she said, but was surprised at how deep her voice sounded. "And the wound is on my side, under my left arm."

"Show me," he repeated slowly, and put his hand on her shoulder.

Her skin sizzled at his touch. It was too much temptation. She nodded and dropped the towel.

Rosie didn't know what to expect. Would he turn away? Every moment the unspoken question hung in the air her passion spun higher. Yet, so help her, she could not have blinked as much as an eyelid if her life had depended on it.

He didn't turn. He didn't budge. He didn't seem to be breathing.

Part of her wanted him to whisk her up and carry her to bed. But the part of her that could've moved stood transfixed as his hand finally…finally…flexed and began caressing her shoulder as he bent to place kisses against her neck.

Even in the shadowed lighting, the sight of his darkly suntanned hand, contrasting against her pale body, was exciting. The skin lying under his fingers grew heated and began to tingle.

He stepped in closer and she could feel his warmth against her back. Her sensitive skin flamed and flushed, igniting at every point they came together. She could also feel the hard ridge under the placket of his jeans zipper poking into the small of her back. The juncture of her thighs flooded with moisture and she watched her own eyes going wide in the mirror.

She opened her mouth to beg, but no sound came out. Wanting to face him, to touch him, she started to turn. But his right hand came up under her arm to her ribcage and pulled her back into his chest.

"Stay," he growled.

He rubbed his palm upward so that his fingers were in position to trace her taut peaks. She moaned. Wanted to squirm. Instead her head fell back against his shoulder as he pulled and lightly pinched her sensitive nipples.

Every movement felt so wonderful. So perfect. Had sex ever been good before? Not like this, she was sure.

Jericho's other hand slid around her hips, flattening against her belly. A downpour of sensation raced straight to the spot between her legs that ached for him, as his hand slowly inched lower through the curly hair under her belly button.

Her eyelids drooped and her knees trembled.

"Watch," he gasped.

Her lids popped open and she stared straight ahead at the sight of the two of them in the mirror. While with one hand he rubbed and provoked the tips of her breasts, his other thumb flicked over her feminine nub—stroking, tempting, tormenting.

The woman in the mirror looked so wanton. She was sensual, heavy-lidded, breathing through an open mouth and with startling rosy nipples that grew higher at every caress.

But as Jericho continued to tighten the string on her reserves, Rosie decided she didn't care how it all looked. She only wanted to experience an end to this growing pull inside her.

"Jericho, please." How sexy she sounded to her own ears. Every movement of Jericho's and every sound she made only served to build the tension higher and higher inside her.

He began murmuring soft words of lust into her ear in that lazy, erotic Texas drawl of his. Stroking and caressing, his fingers worked faster, harder, until she thought her whole body would burst into flame.

At last the tight rubber band inside her snapped in a flood of sensation as the orgasm washed over her. In the mirror, her eyes widened impossibly and her mouth dropped open in a very unfeminine scream.

Pulsating aftershocks hit her in waves of pure pleasure. Her knees buckled and Jericho lifted her into his arms.

He turned to carry her into the bedroom as she whimpered against his chest. This was going to be a long but fantastic night. She couldn't wait.

Chapter 9

"Hang on." Jericho carefully laid her down on the guest bed, flipped on the bedside lamp then turned and strode back out the door.

Hang on? What could he mean, and where was he going?

Rosie's senses still reeled. But she suddenly felt cold without him. He should be here beside her. She needed to touch him and make him feel every bit as good as he'd done for her. Together they were going to be spectacular. So why wasn't he here?

Minutes dragged by before he reappeared in the doorway, carrying something in his hand.

"If you're worried about protection," she began, "I can understand your concern. But the doctor's tests would probably have caught anything I might've had. And if it's for the other reason, wouldn't that be like locking the prison door after the criminals already escaped?"

"Turn on your side." Ignoring her comments, he slid a hand beneath her and urged her to turn on her right side, facing away from him.

Hmm. Was this usual? she wondered. Why couldn't she remember having sex? This was like being a virgin—at least in her mind.

Instead of sliding his body into the bed behind her, he raised her arm above her head and began rebandaging her wound. "This won't take but a minute. Then you can get some sleep."

"What? Aren't you coming to bed with me?" She couldn't see his expression as he worked on her side, but his tight silence told her everything.

"Jericho, I don't want to go to bed alone." She heard the tones of exasperation mingling with her near desperation and tried to calm down. "I want you to come to bed with me so we can finish what we started. You didn't…I mean, you didn't have your…um…turn. Let me touch you. Let me feel you inside me."

Instead of answering, she felt him patting down the edges of the tape around the bandage. Then he gently placed her arm down at her side and turned her over on her back. Staring up at him, Rosie became so frustrated she wanted to scream.

Jericho's eyes gleamed bright with what she would swear must be desire as he gazed down on her naked body. He reached over and placed his palm flat against her belly. The fire his hand caused seared her there and set her aflame once more.

She groaned and reached her arms out to him.

"No." He grimaced but left his wide hand gently but firmly against her flushed skin. "Tucked safely under my hand is someone else we have to consider. We can't just act without thinking through the consequences for everyone. Your child has a father—somewhere.

"I shouldn't have taken advantage of you like that," he went on. "The two of you need to know where you belong—*before* making any decisions you might come to regret. Tonight was all my fault. I've promised to protect you, and I mean to, even if it has to be protection from me."

He took a deep breath. "You've had a bad night. Mostly due to my mistakes. I'd appreciate it if you would sleep now."

Too stunned at his little speech to speak, Rosie blinked up at him as he lifted the covers and tucked her in. This guy was definitely too good. Or was that more like so good it could be bad?

As he turned off the light and backed out the door, she worked to bite back her neediness, closing her eyes and wishing a dream to come for what she really wanted.

But when the images came into her mind, she couldn't tell if they were dreams or not. Everything seemed so familiar. But then again…it might not be her own reality.

The soft evening air, tenderly perfumed with the scent

of flowers, ruffled her hair. The sounds of an orchestra played in the background. Gentle laughter and conversation floated lightly on a sweet breeze.

How strange.

She was floating, too. In a long blue gown. Shimmering up a staircase that appeared out of nowhere. A staircase that looked as though it must belong in a castle.

How amusing. And how thrilling.

Before her appeared a prince. Wearing a tux, his royal bearing quickly became a powerful aphrodisiac. Tall and lean, with dark brown hair combed in an impeccable style, he stood out above all the rest. She felt a tiny pang of regret, somehow missing dark blond hair that grew over the collar and always appeared messy.

But then the prince gave her a generous smile that eased into a deep dimple on his left cheek, and her heart fluttered. Thoughts of any other smiles flittered away as his eyes filled with romance, passion and sex.

The prince held out his hand to her, and she stepped into his arms. Music filled her head with sparkling, erotic diamonds of pure passion as they danced across a ballroom floor like a royal couple.

Was she a princess? Looking down at herself, she saw glass slippers on her feet. So...not a princess. She must be only pretending.

But she quickly decided she didn't care. Twirling around the dance floor, she felt beautiful—and powerful. Like nothing could ever hurt her, and like everyone in the room would want to be her.

A bolt of lightning suddenly shot golden flashes through the ballroom. With the boom of thunder that *followed, spears of panic darted straight into her heart. She gasped, stepping back and holding a hand to her breast to still the fear.*

Glancing at the prince for reassurance, what she saw instead sent chills up her spine. Dark, demon eyes glared at her with fury and hunger.

Sinister.

Evil.

My God. She stumbled back, turned and fled.

The music disappeared and she was barefoot, running through a field of blood. It was after her. The monster was hot on her heels.

Closing in faster and faster.

She had to hide. Ripping at her clothes, she stripped off the gown and streaked through the foggy night. Shivering now, and mewling like a wounded animal, she fell to her knees. But all around her was blood. A sea of it.

The contents of her stomach curdled with nausea as she tried to crawl away. But the simmering scarlet ocean clung to her, dragging her down. Tentacles reached around her body, tugging at her ferociously.

Dragging at her body.

Pulling her further and further down.

Clawing her way up, Rosie forced her eyes to open. Sunshine glittered into the room, nearly blinding her with its welcoming reality. She was safe. Safe in Jericho's guest bedroom.

Thank heaven. The sheets were twisted around her body, a reminder of her nightmare. They clung to her, tying her to the bed.

She fought them off and swung her legs over the side. Trying to clear the last bit of fog from her brain, Rosie stood up, took a deep breath—and nearly doubled over from the nausea.

That must be still part of the dream, right?

In the next moment, she found out that being sick to her stomach was unfortunately very real. She made a mad dash for the bathroom across the hall, praying she would make it in time.

At nearly midday, Jericho hurried his way through morning bathroom chores. He wasn't too sure he would ever again be able to spend much time in his bathroom. Images of what he and Rosie had done together last night surrounded him and punched him in the gut. Trying to shave, he'd felt himself suffocating on the visions he remembered in the mirror.

Dumb. Taking advantage of the situation last night had been a purely dumb-ass move. He'd always imagined himself to have more self-control. Guess not. At least not when it came to Rosie.

In only two days, the woman had gotten under his skin. Having her stay here in his home wasn't smart. Obviously he couldn't be trusted to keep his hands to himself. Maybe this afternoon he would be better off sneaking her over to one of the neighbor's houses to stay the night. If handled properly, the move could easily remain a secret and she should be safe.

Rubbing at a sudden ache in his chest, Jericho braced himself for seeing her again. Was she still asleep? They'd had a late night, which he hadn't done a blessed thing to help. He hoped to hell she'd been getting the rest she needed since then.

Jericho headed for the kitchen and the coffeepot. But before he could even leave the shelter of the hallway, Rosie's voice wafted through the air and met his ears. Coming to a halt, he stood and listened to her speaking softly to the dogs. In another second she began humming, sweet and low in her throat.

A disturbing memory ambushed him. He hadn't awoken to a woman humming in the kitchen since he'd been seven years old. Sharp, edgy memories of growing up and hoping against hope to hear those feminine sounds once more came darting through his conscious mind.

Waking up in his room upstairs at home, sneaking down to peek into his dad's kitchen and praying that Momma would've finally come home. He'd been so sure that any day now she would be back and tell him she'd made a big mistake in leaving him. Despite Daddy forever saying it would never happen.

Dumb again, Jericho told himself while he exhaled heavily and cleared his head. As an adult, he realized that the family had been much better off without his alcoholic mother. *He'd* been better off, too.

Still, what a surprise to suddenly find that aching need had never completely gone away. That it had just been lurking there in his subconscious. Irritated with himself for being so vulnerable, he stuffed the old feelings back into the dark corner of his mind and went into the kitchen to confront all his demons.

"Good morning," Rosie said and looked up at him as

he entered the room. She was sitting on the kitchen floor, trying to coax Shep into drinking water.

God, she was even more beautiful in the light of day than she'd been last night. If that was even possible.

Refusing to just stand and stare at her, he bent on one knee and checked Shep's eyes. They were much clearer and the old dog seemed to recognize his master.

Jericho cleared his throat. "It's nearly noon, but it looks like the day will be good one. The dogs are better."

"Yes." She gently placed Shep's head back down on his dog bed and stood. "I hope that means they're going to make it."

"I think it must. Though Quinn said it would take a couple of days to be sure." He stood too and turned to the coffeepot. "Have you had anything to eat?"

"Uh, no. I fixed myself some tea and made you some coffee. But I'm not really very hungry."

He glanced over his shoulder, really looking at her, and saw that her face was pale, her hair standing up on end as though she'd run her hands through it. "You okay?"

"I had a nightmare. But I think it might mean something. Maybe my memories will be coming back through my dreams. What do you think?"

His first thought, that her returning memory was the last thing he wanted, sideswiped him with unusual force. When she remembered, she would leave him and go back to her life. *Breathe.* After another moment, he got his bearings and mentally kicked himself for being such a fool. Of course she needed to remember. It was her life.

"It's possible," he said. "Doc O'Neal said the memories might come back in bits and pieces." Jericho tried to smile at her, to reassure her, but he didn't feel much like smiling. "What did you dream?"

"Most of it was silly—or scary. But I clearly remember looking down at myself and thinking I looked like a fairy princess. With long, beautiful and shiny hair." She reached up and tugged at her own short locks. "Not the horrible-looking mess that's there now."

He blinked a couple of times and all of sudden the image of her naked in the mirror last night sprang into his head. "You know, I believe you probably are a natural blonde. If that makes you feel any better."

She frowned. "No. That just makes things worse. I want to know for sure. I wish I had a picture. Being sure about my looks might make it easier for the rest of it to come back."

"Well, now," he said as the idea gelled in his mind. "I think we need an expert opinion. And maybe you might discover something you enjoy doing at the same time.

"Get your shoes on. I'll call one of the neighbors to come over and stay with the dogs for the afternoon. I know where we'll find just the person we need to figure it out."

Rosie once again stared intently at herself in a mirror. Only this time the mirror was at Sallie Jo's Cut N Curl, a few doors down from the sheriff's office. The person standing directly behind Rosie with her fingers sliding through Rosie's hair was the owner, Sallie Jo Stanton.

"What do you think, Sal?" Jericho asked from his spot, off to the side. "That red can't be for real. Can you tell anything about the natural color?"

"Hmm." Sallie was a woman in her early forties. Maybe a little heavyset for her bones, but her hair and makeup seemed impeccable and her clothes fit perfectly.

She combed Rosie's hair into sections. "Yeah, looky there. The blond roots are already growing out.

"Now why would you want to cover up your gorgeous ash-blond with that nasty red dye, sugar?"

Rosie lifted her eyebrows. "I don't know—for sure. But can you put it back to natural?"

Sallie shook her head and studied the hair a little closer. "The only way to totally get rid of the dark red color would be too harsh. I could strip it out, but that would ruin your hair and it still wouldn't be natural."

She lifted a section so Rosie could see it clearly in the mirror. "We can lighten it up some. Maybe end up as a strawberry blonde for a while. But the best thing will be to let me cut it shorter so it can grow out quicker."

"Shorter?" Rosie felt positive she should have long hair. All down her back, if she believed in dreams.

"This…I hesitate to call it a cut…isn't doing you any favors, hon." Sallie picked up her shears. "All these split ends and funny angles just call attention to the drastic dye job. Let me style it short for you.

"Think of it this way," Sallie continued as she combed through the hair once again. "Cutting is one way to get rid of that awful coloring job a lot faster. Then we'll lighten the rest and before you know it, you'll be blond again. What do you say?"

"Okay, I guess so."

Jericho stepped into her view in the mirror. "That's fine. You'll be good here for a while, right? I'm going over to speak to the deputy. He needs to revise his bulletin and recheck with the people around the county.

"We've been asking about a redhead when we should've been checking for any word on a blonde." With that, he tipped his hat at Sallie. "I'll be back in a couple of hours. That do?"

"Sure, Sheriff." Sallie watched Jericho leave with an admiring gleam in her eyes. "That there is sure one fine-looking man. If I wasn't already married…" Her voice trailed off, leaving no question what she'd do.

Yes, Jericho surely was fine-looking. And a fine-quality man, too.

Rosie suspected that Jericho would turn out to be the best man she had ever known. Over the last two days, between hiding for her life and almost having sex, she had fallen in love with him. And she had a strong sense that he felt the same way about her. Now all she had to do was prove it to him. There had to be some way to make him see that the two of them belonged together.

Rosie was determined to find it.

Deputy Rawlins checked his watch and discovered it was past five o'clock. It'd been a long, discouraging night last night and he should've been off the clock long ago. But he wanted to make just one more stop before he headed home this afternoon.

He'd already checked with some of the truckers at the truck stop yesterday. But today he had new information.

For fifteen minutes Adam spoke to as many of the drivers as he could find. Finally, he'd found one who claimed to know something.

"Yeah, I gave a ride to a drop-dead gorgeous blonde," the long-haul trucker said. "Five days ago. I have it in my log. A real looker, that one. She'd be hard to forget."

Adam asked for a better description.

"Oh man, hair and legs down to there," the driver said with a grin. "And a shape worth losing your job over— if you know what I mean."

Though not a perfect description, Adam figured it was close enough. "Can you tell me where you picked her up and dropped her off?"

"Sure. I picked her up sixty miles or so north on the interstate. Between Austin and San Antonio. At a joint called Stubbins Barbeque. You ever heard of the place?"

"Yeah," Adam said. He'd eaten there, the place was famous. "The food's good, even if the patrons are on the rowdy side."

The driver nodded. "Don't know that the lady ate anything. I'd eaten earlier, but old Charlie Stubbins lets drivers catch a few hours sleep in the back of his lot. So I was just about to get underway again when I spotted this babe running down the side of the highway. She looked like she'd seen a ghost. I figured a couple hours in the cab with a broad who looked like that wouldn't be such a bad thing. You know?"

Adam nodded, then continued, "Where'd you drop her?"

"I was heading across the border. Let her out just this side of the river, in the town of Rio View."

Adam got the driver's name, address and number, then sent him on his way. Jericho should be pleased with this new info.

At least now they had a handle on where to start looking. All they had left to do was ask a million questions at both ends until something popped.

And at the same time, they'd better keep watch on their backsides for an ambush. Adam didn't like it, but he guessed that this kind of thing was all part of the job.

Chapter 10

The hired gunman called Arnie eased his stolen pickup into the dark lot of a roadside bar near the Mexican border. He found a spot to park on the caliche and got out. At long past the midnight hour, and considering it was during the middle of the week, the place seemed usually packed. Dirty trucks and well-used four-wheel-drive SUVs squeezed into every inch.

Grateful to have already made it over the border and back, Arnie gave a moment's thought to his previous partner. He'd left Petey in that medical clinic in Ciudad Acuna. No one there spoke much English, but the medicos managed to treat Petey's wound and more or less agreed to keep him in the clinic until his arm healed. Arnie had just been glad it was cheap.

Also thankful that their employer had given him another chance, Arnie figured otherwise he would probably be dead right now. But this time around, the boss wanted things to go differently. And whatever the boss wanted, Arnie was willing to do. It would keep him alive a few days longer.

That's why Arnie was about to walk into this rough, sleazy out-of-the-way nightspot. The meeting had been set up for 1:00 a.m., and Arnie hoped to hell he managed to leave by 2:00 a.m. with both a new partner and a new plan. Most of all, he hoped to get out of the place alive and in one piece. If this turned out to be a setup, he would never know what hit him.

Inside, after his eyes got used to the low lighting, Arnie spotted the man he was supposed to meet. Located at a table in a dimly lit corner, the guy was sitting with his back to the wall. A group of dangerous-looking hangers-on surrounded him, leaning their elbows on his table. A chill ran up Arnie's spine as the man in the middle of things tilted his head and shot him a narrowed-eyed stare across the smoky room.

He'd seen this man before, of course. In a much different context. But even tonight in this backwater bar, the guy carried an air of respect. His dark brown hair had not a strand out of place. His lips turned up in a kind of sneer as his eyes followed Arnie's movements. But when Arnie got closer he saw that a dimple marred the strength in the man's craggy cheek. A shift in the guy's position at the table as he raised his bottle of beer caused a small beam of light to glint against the metal badge affixed to his breast pocket.

Swallowing his fear, Arnie gathered his courage as he strode through the crowds. It was too late to ask how he'd gotten himself into this.

Too late to do anything differently either. Arnie braced himself for the worst—and hoped to hell it would end with the best.

Rosie awoke sick to her stomach again the next morning. But she was no longer in Jericho's guest bedroom. Despite her protests, last night he had delivered her to his best friend's Bar None ranch for the night. Clay Colton and Tamara Brown were lovely hosts, but they simply could never replace the man she loved.

Rolling out of bed, she tiptoed into the guest bath and lost whatever was left of the contents of her stomach. Today's morning sickness was a big fat reminder of yesterday. But similar as it was, last night there had been no dreams. Not even one fuzzy glimpse of her past. She wondered if that was because she was no longer in close proximity to Jericho. Perhaps he was the catalyst for her returning memories. If so, that might be a good excuse to stay near him.

Washing her face and brushing her teeth, Rosie couldn't help feeling somewhat lost without the security of Jericho nearby. This morning Tamara had promised to take her shopping for clothes at a mall she frequented just this side of San Antonio. But afterward Rosie was scheduled to spend the rest of the day with Jericho, trying to trace her movements on the days before she lost her memory.

Checking out her new hairdo in the bathroom mirror,

Rosie was pleased with what she saw. The stylish cut and lighter color made her look almost sophisticated. Sallie had given her a little makeup, too, and as she applied a touch of lip gloss a picture began to form in her mind.

A picture of herself, in a dark gray business suit and crisp white blouse, getting ready for work. So…she must have a job. But if she did, why hadn't her boss reported her missing?

Why hadn't *anyone* reported her missing? Didn't she even have any friends that missed her?

Becoming frustrated once again, Rosie put away all her unanswerable questions and finished getting dressed. If that's the way her old life had been—no friends, a boss who didn't care if she showed up, and a husband or boyfriend who couldn't be bothered to report her missing—then she didn't want to remember.

She decided not to buy anything that looked like a business suit today when they went shopping. Getting something that was right for Esperanza, Texas—and its sheriff—would be a much better way to go.

Jericho helped Rosie up into the passenger seat of his pickup. Since he'd showed up here at Clay's ranch to pick her up a few minutes ago, he couldn't seem to take his eyes off her. She looked so different with the new haircut and new clothes that really fit.

Not bad, mind you. But different. Spectacular.

The bruises around her face had nearly disappeared, and it looked as though the long, lean woman had evolved into a real Texas stunner in her narrow dark jeans and a tight-fitting denim jacket. She seemed to belong at one of those big outdoor Texas-style charity events, held in Dallas or Houston, rather than in small-town Esperanza, Texas. She wasn't the Rosie he had been getting to know over the last few days.

But then, who was she?

"Where are we going first, Jericho?"

To find out who you really are so I can know who I'm falling in love with. "To Stubbins Barbeque. It's about sixty miles up the road. Ever heard of it?"

She put her thumbnail to her lips, lost in thought.

"For a moment…I thought…" She shook her head. "No, it doesn't sound familiar. But then nothing does. Why are we going there?"

"Someone said they thought they saw you at the place almost a week ago. I want to ask around now that your hair is lighter and see if anyone recognizes you. Okay?"

She squirmed a little in her seat. But when she turned to answer, her eyes were bright and she had a big, warm smile on her lips. "Great. Wouldn't it be terrific if we find someone who knows me?"

Past the words— Past the smile—

There was a sense of misery about her. When he looked deeper, he noticed a tiny lick of fear hiding in those brilliant blue eyes. If she was miserable because their time together might be drawing to an end, that was okay. He felt much the same way.

But the fear—now, that bothered him. He intended to protect her from those goons or any others sent in their place. Didn't she know that? What else was there for her to be afraid about?

Confused, but determined to stand beside her despite

whatever they might uncover, Jericho headed his truck up the ramp to the interstate and drove on toward the answers.

As they turned off I-35 at the exit for Stubbins restaurant, Rosie's nerves tensed and strained. Nothing looked even vaguely familiar. Still, the closer they drove down the frontage road, the more jittery she became.

"Any sparks of recall?" Jericho asked as he turned onto the gigantic blacktop parking lot.

The smells of mesquite smoke mixed with her panic and filled the air with doubts.

Yes. "No. Maybe." She rubbed at the hairs standing up on her arms. "Nothing specific. Just a bad feeling."

"I'm right here. But don't do anything that makes you too uncomfortable. Just let me know and we'll leave."

Jericho parked behind the big red barn of a building, turned off the pickup and rounded the truck to help her down. "Ready?"

Rosie felt as if she were being marched to the guillotine. "I guess so. What are we going to do?"

"We're going to find out if anyone remembers seeing you on the first of the month. That's when the driver claims he picked up a blonde."

"But…" The sign beside the entryway said the hours were noon to midnight. All the deputy had managed to get was a date. How many people had come and gone on that day?

Jericho took her hand and strode up to the cashier's booth. The woman behind the counter was bleached blond, skinny as a rail and watched them with sharp, hawklike eyes.

She coughed and cleared her throat before picking up a couple of paper placemats and raising her painted-on eyebrows. "Just the two of you?" she asked with what sounded like a smoker's rasp.

Jericho shook his head. "I'm Sheriff Yates from Campo County. We're investigating a shooting, and I'd like to speak to anyone who was working here on the first of this month."

The cashier looked a little taken aback, but she glared at his badge and the gun strapped in its holster at his side before she said, "A shooting *here,* Sheriff?"

"*Was* there a shooting here on that date?"

"We've had our share of knife fights and an occasional gunshot," she said by way of an answer. "But not last week. I worked that day—the lunch shift."

"I would imagine I need to talk to someone working later in the day. Could you tell us who worked the dinner shift?"

Rosie quietly tried to stem her unease. She shifted from one foot to the other and folded her arms under her breasts.

"Let me check." The cashier pulled a plastic-covered chart out from under the counter and studied it for a moment. "There's two waiters and a busboy who were here that night and who'll also be on tonight. Actually, they might be already in back getting set to start their shift. If they're here, I'll send them on out.

"Besides them," she added. "I'll have to check with the manager to see if I can give you a list of the others who worked that night."

The cashier asked them to wait and they stood in the small lobby, idly staring at framed pictures of prize bulls that sported blue ribbons and snorted at the camera. Rosie found it hard to think. She couldn't even manage to get a word to form.

A young man with dark hair and a big apron came out of the open half of the kitchen and walked up to them. The kid looked scared to death of Jericho, but he stood his ground and answered questions.

After one look at Rosie, though, he shook his head. "So sorry," the kid mumbled with a heavy Spanish accent before he went back to work.

Another young man, this one with his light brown hair tied back in a thong at the nape of his neck and wearing jeans, a checked shirt and a red vest that obviously was part of his uniform, stepped out of another back room. He immediately seemed to recognize her.

"Hey," he said. "You cut your hair. Shame. It was cool all the way down your back like that."

"You've seen me before?"

"Sure. You were in the other night with another woman. Older broad. Maybe your grandma? Don't you remember me?" He went on as if he didn't expect an answer. "I remember the two of you paid in cash. Not something we see a lot around here what with truck drivers and business people using credit cards and all. You two weren't bad tippers, either…for two single women."

A picture of an older woman who looked something like Becky French, only she was wearing a business suit, glasses and a worried expression, flashed in and out of Rosie's mind. She started to sweat. Trying hard, she couldn't bring back anything more.

Jericho asked the young man another question or

two but suddenly Rosie's ears were ringing. Her legs became spongy and she found herself leaning on the sheriff for support.

He slung his arm around her waist, thanked the waiter and pulled her outside into the sunshine. "What's wrong with you? Aren't you feeling well?"

"Something…" One look around the parking lot and a flood of images flashed in her brain like a movie on fast-forward.

Darkness and fear. Someone chasing her across the blacktop. A gunshot. A thud from behind her.

Blinded by fear, she couldn't breathe. "Ahhh." The muffled scream came unbidden from Rosie's mouth but it originated somewhere deep, primal. "Is she hurt? I have to run. Hide."

Suddenly Jericho had her in his arms, rocking her gently. "You're okay. What do you remember? Who was hurt?"

She couldn't stop trembling and found herself shaking her head as though that might clear up the images. "I…I can't make it come back." The tears started to flow. "For a second back there, I saw another woman sitting across the table. A friend, I think. But now I can't…the pictures in my mind won't come back."

"What about out here in the parking lot?"

Swiping furiously at her cheeks in frustration, Rosie glanced around the lot. "It's just bits and pieces. Something that sounded like a gunshot—or maybe a car back-firing. Dark shapes moving through the shadows. Damn. Why can't I remember?"

Jericho half dragged her over to his truck, opened the

door and helped her in. "Stay here. Lock the doors and stay put. I'm going back for a couple more questions then we'll head out. You'll be okay?"

She nodded her head. But without her memories, she wasn't sure she would ever really be okay again.

Jericho spent the next half hour talking to the manager of the restaurant and then driving himself and Rosie over to the local county sheriff's office. He'd only met the newly elected sheriff of this county, Richard Benway, once. But had heard Benway was a good man.

Rosie's color had come back by the time they finished at the sheriff's office. It had been decided that Benway would open a full investigation as to what exactly had taken place in the restaurant's parking lot on the night of July first.

Jericho had loads of unanswered questions. The truck driver who picked up Rosie hadn't seen another woman, so what happened to her? Had she been hurt? Had anyone witnessed what took place? And how exactly had Rosie arrived at the restaurant in the first place? Driven? If so, what happened to her car?

Luckily, Sheriff Benway was willing to do the legwork. He had the authority and the extra manpower. But there were no guarantees the investigation would be successful.

Back in the truck, Rosie turned to him and asked, "What's next? Are we going home?"

It was a shock to his system to hear her calling Esperanza home. But he found he sort of liked it.

"This time of year," he began easily. "The sun doesn't

set until nearly 9:00 p.m. I thought we could drive on to the border. Check out the town where the truck driver says he let you out.

"You willing to give it a try?" he added thoughtfully. "Are you too tired?"

"I'm okay. If there's any chance of finding out who I am by going, then I'm there."

Jericho nodded and pushed down on the accelerator. This time they would play it smarter and start at the county sheriff's office.

But, unfortunately, he knew this county's sheriff. Knew him only too well.

There'd been rumors for years about how Sheriff Jesus Montalvo had gotten rich by turning his back to the forty-mile stretch of border that his county shared with Mexico. Like Jericho, Montalvo's county had no big cities and a small tax base. But unlike Jericho, Sheriff Montalvo of San Javier County had managed to accumulate an enormous amount of land and a few heavy bank accounts. The only difference between counties was a wild forty miles of Rio Grande riverfront.

Still, Montalvo *would* help. He had a large staff of deputies and knew where all the bodies and secrets were buried in his territory.

By the time they arrived in Rio View it was suppertime. Rosie didn't think she was hungry until her stomach started rumbling and she remembered that she hadn't eaten anything today. Jericho called ahead and Sheriff Montalvo agreed to meet them at a truck-stop restaurant near where the truck driver had claimed he'd let Rosie off late on the night of the first.

As they entered the crowded diner, that same uneasy feeling from before began to niggle around the edges of Rosie's mind. She forced it aside, determined this time to either ignore the images and feelings or capture them whole and place them properly in her memory.

A waitress pointed out the booth where Sheriff Montalvo was waiting. They worked their way through the loaded tables and past row upon row of full booths made with brown plastic seats and linoleum-covered tables. Everywhere Rosie looked were men. Long-haul truck drivers. Cowboys and ranchers. Rugged-looking men who seemed too busy eating to pay much attention.

Until…she walked by. Then every set of eyes studied her carefully. It gave her the creeps.

She'd thought she would be glad to slip into the booth across from Sheriff Montalvo and get away from the stares. But when she came near enough to the table to get a good look, there was something about him that seemed darkly familiar.

Not knock-you-down familiar. But close.

The man sat slouched in the far corner of the booth, but the power of his position glowed around him. He wasn't wearing a hat and his brown hair was combed in a perfect style. His white shirt looked starched and crisp under his badge.

A couple of waitresses stood beside the booth, like two virginal handmaidens. Rosie could just tell that everyone in the place, probably everyone in the county, would treat this sheriff with deference.

She grew uneasy again. Did she know this man? And if so, would he be able to tell her who she was?

Easing her way into the booth in front of Jericho, Rosie suddenly surprised herself by wishing that Sheriff Montalvo would not be able to tell her a blessed thing.

Chapter 11

"Is it very far from here?" Rosie stared out the windshield into the growing silver-gray dusk.

Jericho watched her body tensing with every mile they drove and his gut twisted from wanting to do something for her. Montalvo hadn't turned out to be of much help. The San Javier County sheriff told them he hadn't gotten any reports of trouble or missing women. But something about Montalvo's body language had been saying that he at least knew of Rosie, though he swore he'd never laid eyes on her before.

As they'd waited for their supper, Montalvo prompted Jericho and Rosie to ask around the restaurant to see if anyone recognized her. No one did. But Jericho's instincts had screamed at him through the whole search. The diner crowd had looked at her with hints of recognition in their eyes, yet not one would even meet his gaze with their own as he'd been asking questions. Liars.

After supper, Montalvo had also encouraged him to check with a motel on the outskirts of town that might match Rosie's description of the one she'd seen on the day she had lost her memory. Montalvo even called ahead to get them an appointment with the manager/owner.

As they pulled up in front, Jericho decided Rosie's original description fit the place perfectly. A cheap motel on the poorer side of a small border town. Just as she'd described it.

The deepening purple shadows of nightfall obscured his view of Rosie's face as they walked to the motel office. But he could feel the nervous energy radiating from her.

At the office door, he stood still for a moment, holding on to the handle as the fluorescent light from inside shone out through the glass. "Something's coming back to you, isn't it?"

Her eyes were wide and bright and her face flushed. "This is the place," she whispered. "From that morning when those two goons grabbed me. I remember the neighborhood."

"Yeah. I figured it was. Anything else coming back?"

She shook her head and bit her lip.

"Okay, let's see what we can find out from the owner." He let her go in ahead of him so he could watch the reaction of the man behind the desk.

The owner turned out to be a portly guy in his fifties, dressed in shorts and a T-shirt turned gray from washing. The bald spot on the man's head was almost covered over by several thin ash-brown strands of hair. But not quite. From Jericho's viewpoint, towering over the man's five-foot-eight frame, the guy would've been a lot better off leaving the bare patch alone.

As they stepped into the room, the owner never blinked an eyelash or showed any recognition of Rosie. But then once they came closer, Jericho caught a glimpse of the man's pupils widening involuntarily at the sight of her—right before he quickly glanced away. The man knew her all right. Even if he wasn't going to admit it.

They introduced themselves. The motel owner seemed put out at having to answer questions. Too bad.

"So, you're sure you don't recognize this woman?" Jericho asked after the man had just said he didn't. "Take another look."

"Once is plenty, bud. The answer is no. Back off."

Jericho lost it in that instant. He grabbed the owner by the front of his shirt and lifted him off his feet and halfway over the counter.

"It's Sheriff Yates to you, *bud*. And Sheriff Montalvo said you would cooperate. Let's have some of that cooperation right now.

"This woman was here in your motel no more than four days ago. Take a better look."

"Jericho…" Rosie put her hand on his shirtsleeve and her expression said she didn't want this much trouble.

Jericho lowered the owner back to his feet but refused

to open his fist. In fact, he still held the man's shirtfront in a death grip.

"Oh…oh, yeah," the owner stuttered as he took another look at Rosie. "Ya see, I didn't recognize you. You've changed. You're the broad that had the long, blond hair.

"You left one hell of a mess in the bathroom of one of the units when you dashed outta here, you know? There was hair and blackish-red dye everywhere. Ruined a couple of our good towels, I can tell you that."

Jericho let him go and then threw a couple of bucks from his pocket onto the counter. "That should take care of any damages.

"Was she registered here?" he added, putting a demanding tone in his words. "Under what name?"

The guy shrugged. "I don't remember. Or, maybe I just wasn't on duty when she came in."

"You want to take a look at the register anyway?" Jericho's patience with this character was running thin.

After another ten minutes of avoiding giving any actual answers, the owner shrugged again and said, "Look, we're not in the business of asking questions about our guests. This place isn't located on any main highway. The people that come here do it for their privacy."

"And I suppose your guests all pay in cash?" Jericho was ready to pound this sucker into the ground if he hedged one more time.

"Sure. In advance. We don't take credit cards and only take checks from the people that live around here."

"Well…" Frustration was making Jericho steamy. "How did she arrive then? Not on foot, surely."

The manager narrowed his eyes at Jericho. "None of my business. There's a bus stop about a block down. Maybe that way. How should I know? Ask her."

Jericho's hands fisted once again, but just then Rosie touched his shoulder. "This isn't doing any good," she told him. "I'm not getting any flashes of my past here. Let's just go."

"Hey," the manager said as he tilted his head to give her another look. "What're all the questions for? Don't you remember?"

The way he had said it told Jericho the man already knew very well that Rosie couldn't remember her past. And probably knew why not. Someone had already told him. Or warned him. Sheriff Montalvo? The sheriff was the only one who could've let the owner know what was going on.

If that was the case, then Rosie was right. They weren't going to get anything else out of this guy. In fact, all of a sudden it seemed like he'd had been deliberately hedging his answers in order to keep them here longer. If the sheriff were somehow involved, then whatever was going on in Rio View and with Rosie went far beyond danger-ous. It would have to involve something bigger and more secretive than just a woman who'd been kidnapped.

Jericho's gut was telling him he needed to get Rosie out of San Javier County. Fast.

"Let's go." He took her by the arm and rushed them both outside and into his truck.

Buckling up, Jericho mentally ticked off the various routes he could take that would get them back to Esperanza the quickest. Menacing darkness began closing in around the pickup as he pulled out of the motel parking lot and kept an eye on what was going on in the rearview mirror.

Rosie cast a sideways glance at Jericho's profile in the glow of the dashboard lights. His jaw was set and a slight tick pulsed under his right eye. The man must still be furious.

She had never seen him as mad as he'd been while he questioned the motel owner. He'd controlled it in the office as long as she stood by his side, but the whole time she'd been afraid that the thin string binding up his anger would snap at any moment.

But why should he still be mad? He had no reason to be mad at her. She couldn't help it if her memories were lost. Yet he seemed furious.

With no clue as to what he was thinking, she looked out the pickup's window as the few remaining buildings on the outskirts of Rio View flew past. Rosie noted that they'd begun picking up speed. When the city-limits sign sped by and nothing but black, moonless night took the place of outdoor floodlights and lighted billboard signs, she all of a sudden realized they were zipping down the highway way too fast. Good thing the roads seemed deserted at this hour.

She cast a quick look over to the speedometer and was stunned to see the gage touching the ninety mark. Asphalt rushed under the truck as she tightened her seat belt. She was not ready to die tonight just because Jericho was a little miffed.

"What's wrong?" she asked him, and was embarrassed by the squeak in her voice. "Are you mad at me?"

"No."

Well, at least he'd answered. But that wasn't enough of an explanation for her. "Then what's up with you?"

It was then that she finally noticed him checking the rearview mirror every few seconds. "Someone is following us." She'd answered her own question.

He shot her a sideways glance then went back to concentrating on the road ahead. "Not yet."

"Yet? How do you know for sure that…"

"Crap." Jericho must've stepped down harder on the gas pedal just then because the truck gave a roar, bucked and unbelievably the speedometer needle eased up past one hundred. "There they are."

Rosie twisted her neck so she could look out the rear window. About a half a mile back a set of headlights could be seen in the distance heading in their same direction.

"What makes you think that car is following us?"

"Gut feeling. That guy in the motel kept us there for far too long. He set us up."

"Well, what do they want?"

Jericho spared her one, quick glare. "Guess."

"Me? Oh, God." Her voice almost left her in the dust as the truck flew down the highway into the dark. "What are we going to do?" she rasped out.

"We're going to lose them."

But even through those determined words, Rosie could hear the other vehicle's engine roaring up right behind them. She turned again and saw a huge set of headlights bearing down on them. They were close. Too close. How had they caught up so fast?

"All we need is another mile…" Jericho's words were interrupted by a loud thump and a terrific jerk.

"They're ramming us," Rosie screamed.

Were they crazy? Ramming people while doing a hundred miles an hour could get them all killed.

While Jericho struggled with the wheel, downshifted then hit the gas again, Rosie turned back to see the other vehicle losing ground. Apparently they'd had to fight the effects of the bump themselves.

"There it is." Jericho tapped the brake, cranked the wheel in a ninety-degree angle and downshifted into second. The engine whined and the tires squealed, but the truck responded in a perfectly executed wheelie, hitting the hidden side road back on all fours.

Rosie thought her lungs would explode. The truck barreled down a narrow paved road with barbed-wire fence whizzing by on both sides. She gasped for breath, closed her eyes and hung on.

"Do you know where you're going?" Blinking open her eyes, she screeched past the engine's whine. This might turn out to be a dead end. Then what would they do?

Jericho was keeping one eye on the rearview mirror as he answered, "My dad and I used to hunt the leases in this section. If nothing's changed since then, I know every inch. There's a couple of places to lose them up ahead."

If nothing's changed? That might be a big if when their lives depended on it. Rosie shivered and prayed for all she was worth.

Jericho drove on through the darkened fields, forced to continue using his headlights and pushing his truck as much as he dared. But they hadn't gone far enough to be safe when he picked up the other guy's headlights once again in his rearview mirror.

Finally spotting what he'd been waiting for, he slowed just enough to make the turn onto a caliche farm-to-market road. The tires clanged over a cattle guard and spun briefly before they caught again. Stepping down on the gas after the truck righted, he noted that the fencing was gone from the left side of the roadway. *Open range.* Dangerous driving in the dark.

Figuring they had about five miles to go before they made cover in the woods just past Gage's Arroyo crossing, he hoped to hell they made it that far.

Jericho threw a fast glance toward Rosie and vowed they would make it, at least that far—and beyond. The other choice was unthinkable. Once they hit the woods he would find some place to hide the truck, for long enough to call for help. But that was presuming his cell would work out here. He counted on those woods being located in the next county over. A county with a sheriff he could depend on to come to their aide.

Taking his eyes off the road for a millisecond, he checked on the woman sitting next to him. Her body was stiff. Her breath coming in short staccato bursts, and her fists bunched and ready to strike. He approved. She was scared but ready to fight.

That was his girl. Beautiful as always, but tough when she needed to be. Good for her.

The road got rougher, and he peered out as far as his headlight beams would reach. Pockmarks, potholes and deep ruts kept his speed down to a roar as the truck behind them began gaining ground.

Holding his breath and gritting his teeth against the violent shaking from his truck, Jericho hit the gas again. The next time he looked into the rearview mirror, he'd gained a little ground.

Son of a gun, that was one gigantic mother of a truck. Taller, wider and faster than Jericho's, the thing loomed out of the darkness like a huge beast with blazing eyes. Resembling a fantasy dragon in this darkness, from a distance it even appeared to be snorting smoke out its sides as dust and caliche spewed from under the tires.

He wasn't sure if that description was bad news or good. Bad news because he couldn't outrun them. Good news because he should be able to outmaneuver them on the narrow, slippery back roads.

Wondering if the driver was more, or less, familiar with this range road than he was, Jericho fought the wheel as he tried to bring their surroundings into better focus. Where were they now? How far from the bridge?

There should be a couple of bends in the road up ahead where the packed caliche wound around the edge of a deep arroyo off to his left. He blinked and stared into the star-filled night, trying to judge how far.

At the distant edge of his headlight beams and seemingly right in the middle of the road, he caught the shadow of a mesquite tree. That told him the first bend in the road was coming up. Downshifting enough to take the curve on four wheels, Jericho held his breath waiting for the second curve.

"Jericho, watch out!"

Rosie must've seen the hulking outlines in the road a second before he did. A half dozen cattle had wandered out onto the caliche and were lying around soaking up the day's lingering warmth. Son of a bitch!

Jericho jerked on the wheel and went right, knowing the arroyo was to the left. And hoping against hope to miss any more of the cattle that might be off to that side.

The minute the pickup was off-road, it skidded in the sandy dirt and he lost control. The truck did a one-eighty all by itself. He hung on to the wheel anyway, stepped lightly on the brake and prayed for a clear path.

But tonight they were not going to be so lucky. Out of the darkness loomed a hefty-sized cactus. Dead ahead.

He slammed down on the brake, holding out his right arm in a vain attempt to keep Rosie backed into her seat. But it was too little, too late as the truck's momentum pushed them forward.

In the next instant, he heard his front bumper crunching against the cactus, and the truck came to an abrupt halt, though his body was still violently jolting in the seat. He vaguely heard the air bags deploy—immediately after his head smacked hard against the driver's-side window.

Then it was suddenly all over. Pain shot through his temple and everything faded to black.

Chapter 12

Rosie fought her way around the deflating passenger air bag, coughing at the dust in the air and battling with her seat belt. She scrambled over the center console to reach Jericho's side. His moans, coming from behind the driver's wheel, meant he must be alive. She was okay, so he should be all right. He just had to be.

Everything had gone so quiet. The truck's engine was still running, but it had stopped whining. When she reached Jericho, his inert body took the breath from her lungs with fear. She quickly checked him over and placed her ear to his chest. He wasn't conscious, but he also wasn't bleeding. His breathing seemed heavy but nevertheless steady. Thank heaven.

Just then she heard another noise that sent chills

running down her spine. Leaning over, she turned off the engine, listening intently. Yes, it was the other truck, and it was getting closer.

She tried to keep her head. What should she do? Run into the night and hide? But what about Jericho? She would never, ever leave him here, and there was no way she could carry or drag him away in time.

Without really thinking it all the way through, but minus a moment to consider, Rosie unbuckled Jericho's seat belt. That left her room to undo the safety cover on his holster. She carefully lifted his service weapon from its place, and tried to remember everything she'd learned from him about guns.

Stepping out of the pickup, she faced the road the same way they'd come and listened as the other truck's engine noise got louder and louder.

"Jericho?" she whispered, turning her face to him and silently begging him to wake up and take over for her.

But his soft moan told her that wasn't to be.

Standing in what she hoped was relative safety behind the pickup's open door, and holding Jericho's gun with both hands, Rosie pointed it in the direction of the oncoming engine noise. In the next instant, headlights caught her in their glare as the huge truck navigated the first curve. Petrified, but determined to save both Jericho and herself, she aimed right above the headlights and held her breath.

Hold off, she cautioned herself. Let them get a little closer. That's what Jericho would do.

But Rosie could see that the truck was already slowing and turning more directly toward her as they no doubt had seen Jericho's headlights off the road. There wasn't going to be enough time for perfect shots.

She fired. But must've missed them. They were still coming. Firing once again, she heard a ping and knew that this time she'd at least hit the body of the truck.

That ended up being her last shot because right then the driver apparently caught sight of the cattle in the road. To avoid Rosie's bullets coming from his right and to miss colliding with ten tons of cow dead ahead, the driver dragged his wheel hard to his left.

For a moment or two more, Rosie could see headlights bumping off the road away from her. And then all of a sudden they disappeared. Disappeared!

After a crashing noise that sounded truly terrible to her ears, another unholy silence filled the air. Then, at last, Jericho called her name. She turned and scrambled back to his side.

"Who was doing the shooting?" he asked weakly as he shook his head and fought to untangle his own deflated air bag.

She heaved a deep sigh, so glad he was conscious and seemingly okay that she almost wept. "Me." Holding out his gun to show him, she began to shake. "Are you injured badly? What hurts?"

He gave her a curious look, took the gun and then turned to stare out the window past the cactus. "I'm okay. Where's the other truck?"

"I don't know. After they spotted the cows, the driver went off on the other side of the road. Then I heard a crash."

"The arroyo is over that way," Jericho said darkly. "It

was pretty damned steep and rough down in that spot the last time I saw it."

"Do you think they're still alive?"

Once again, Jericho's answer scared her. "It doesn't matter right now. We have to get out of here. This is still San Javier County. We're in danger every moment we stay here.

"I wonder if my pickup will still run," he added as he put his gun back in the holster, buckled his seat belt and straightened up in his seat.

"I turned it off," she told him. "And the motor was still going then."

He cranked the ignition and it roared to life. "Buckle up again, sweetheart. We're getting out of here. Only this time at a slightly safer speed."

"But shouldn't we check on…whoever that was? Maybe they need help."

"I'm real proud of the way you stood up to those bozos," Jericho said as he put the truck into Reverse and eased backward. "But you don't go sticking your hand in the hole, wondering if the rattlesnakes are doing okay. If they're still alive, that's the last place you should go. If they're not… Well, we'll call the sheriff in the next county and let him find out. Just as soon as we make it there safely ourselves."

Jericho listened from the bedroom of their suite at the bed-and-breakfast as water began running behind the closed bathroom door. Rosie was preparing to take her shower while he tried to sort through his emotions. It had been a very long night so far.

Thankfully, the sheriff in this county was an old friend and had been ready and willing to help. A crew of deputies was dispatched to Gage's Arroyo in the middle of the night to search for survivors. But when they'd found the smashed monster truck at the bottom of the dry arroyo bed, the driver and any passengers had been missing. The questions now seemed centered on whether any survivors had left the scene under their own power or had been thrown clear in the crash. A better search of the area would have to wait until daylight.

Meanwhile, Jericho could hardly arouse any real interest in those bastards. It was Rosie and his feelings toward her that had been hogging all his thoughts.

His old friend Sam Trenton, the sheriff of this county, had seen how beat up and tired he and Rosie had looked after all the questions were answered to the best of their abilities. Sam had called around and found them this one lone vacant suite in an entire county full of summer tourists who'd come for an arts-and-crafts festival.

Driving for a few hours to Esperanza had been out of the question. The pickup would run, but the tires were completely shot, the air bags needed to be replaced, the right front fender was crumpled and the headlight broken.

And the two of them needed rest.

From behind the bathroom door, the sound of running water changed over to the stronger noise of shower spray. Jericho sat down on the edge of the bed to consider what was going to happen when Rosie came out of the bathroom and they found themselves exhausted and alone together in a room with only a king-size bed and a sitting room with one tiny sofa.

His life had changed forever in one intense moment back there on that dark road. Gone was the guy he had once been, the one who'd wanted nothing more out of his life than a bachelor's existence. In his place was a man who would give anything to trade in his old ways for a chance at one red-hot lady who couldn't remember her baby's father. A lady who also easily remembered her weapons' training and thought nothing of wielding a weapon when backed into a corner.

For the last couple of hours, while he'd been checked over in a local clinic and had taken his own shower, he'd found himself thinking not about bad guys but about how best to remodel his cabin. How to change the house he'd built into a real home.

He looked over to the bathroom door. She was there— just on the other side. The only woman he'd ever met for whom he would gladly give up the rest of his life.

For her and for her child. He'd been thinking of her little one, too. More than anything, he wanted to be that child's father. He would make a great dad. He'd had the best example in the world.

For some reason, Jericho discovered he wasn't afraid of Rosie leaving him. Always before, when he'd come close to a serious relationship with a woman, he would call a halt to things sooner rather than later. Mostly due to his worrying about how long it would last before the woman up and left. Maybe that kind of thing was a legacy from his damned mother.

But not this time. If Rosie hadn't left him unconscious in the truck to save herself, and she certainly had not, he was positive she would never leave him at all. Not once she fully committed.

So that was what he was sitting here thinking about. How to go about making her *want* to stay as much as he wanted to keep her. But as usual, whenever he thought of her, the testosterone took over and he quit using his brain altogether.

In fact, right this minute his pulse pounded with need and his senses were on overdrive just knowing she was naked on the other side of that door.

Then with no warning, the door opened and Rosie stood on the threshold to the bedroom wearing nothing but a towel. Like a zombie he stumbled toward her with his arms outstretched.

Those brilliant sapphire eyes of hers swam with need, but she held out one arm to fend off his advance. "Jericho, wait. We have to think this through. I may be a terrible person. At the very least, I'm probably a thief. And obviously I slept with someone who didn't care enough about me to look when I went missing."

"You are my fantasy." It was all he could think to say. "The one I've waited for all my life." He took another step closer.

She backed into the bathroom. "But getting involved with me might bring you lots more trouble. Someone is still after me."

"Too late," he murmured. "I'm already involved. You stayed. You stayed and I don't care who or what you were before. I'll find a way to protect you from anything.

"And what's more," he added with a deep breath. "I hope we never find out who you were."

Her eyes went wide and she dropped the towel, holding out her arms to beckon him closer. It was all the invitation he would ever want.

She was stunning and he was breathless as he dragged her into his arms and pushed them both up against the bathroom counter. He slanted his mouth over hers and stroked her waiting tongue with his own.

Kissing like this, with him half dressed and her totally naked was pure torture. But also pure pleasure. His senses soared as he touched her everywhere. He craved her like a thirsty man craved drink.

Bringing a hand up to caress her breast, he reveled in the soft, weighty feel of it in his palm. She had such fabulous breasts. The joy of touching them intensified. His blood fired as he bent his head and took one rosy tip into his mouth.

She moaned and bucked against his hips. It was such a luxurious gift to hear her moaning under his touches and kisses. He spent another indulgent moment in licking and sucking her deep into his mouth, while at the same time letting his other hand slip easily between her legs to cup her.

Another moan came from her parted lips, and he lifted his head to kiss her again. To swallow her little sounds of pleasure and to push his tongue deep inside her, mimicking what he wanted them to be doing in other ways. He held her tight and felt himself growing harder.

Jericho wanted this to happen, more than he'd ever thought possible. But he also wanted to go slow. To draw out every precious moment—for both of them.

Nibbling his way down the satiny column of her

neck, he found her so sweet-smelling and fresh after her shower, and so compelling with her moist skin and soft moans that it nearly threw him off. He steeled himself against a too-soon ending to all this intimacy.

Rosie felt damned good under his hands, and he wanted her to experience something so special with him that she would never forget it. He needed to become familiar with every inch of her body. It seemed imperative to learn everything that she liked. What turned her on. What brought out those tiny mewling sounds of pleasure. What caused her to jump and shove her hips hard up against him, begging for more.

His fingers sought the nub to her core and rubbed there gently. Testing, exploring. Finally, teasing and tormenting.

"Jericho." His name came out like a whispered prayer. He was so turned on he almost missed that she was starting to come.

Crying out, she buried her hands in his hair and hung on. Her breathing came in short pants. He pulsed with anticipation next to her and gave an instant's thought to slowing her down just to bring her up again.

But in the next moment, when her body went taut and she jerked against him with a whimper, he knew this was so much better. To be able to watch her come apart in his arms was the ultimate pleasure. He'd done it once before but this time was even sweeter. This time there would be another and, he hoped, even another chance to make this happen. They had the time and he definitely had the desire.

Rosie trembled, clutching at him as he lifted her chin and kissed her. Kept on kissing her and touching her and rubbing up against her until she groaned again and reached down for his zipper.

"Please, don't leave me again," she whispered hoarsely as she fumbled with the button on his jeans. *"Please."*

He heard all the words she didn't say. *Come inside me. Become one with me. This is meant to be. I will never leave you.*

Helping her out, he slid out of his boots and shed his jeans while she leaned her bottom against the bathroom counter and watched him from under heavy lids. Then he was there. All for her.

Lifting her hips, he filled her. Pushing deep. Her head leaned back on a moan and her hips jerked forward, shoving him ever deeper.

She gripped his shoulders as he thrust once… twice…until his head was literally spinning. Her internal muscles tightened around him, clenching and stroking. Her body pulled at him, drawing him, locking them together in a primitive way and making sure he stayed with her.

Oh, he would stay with her, all right. Stilling, he looked down at her beautiful face, with her eyelids half-closed and with an expression that said she was lost in sensation. Her lips were parted and her breathing shallow.

Breathing deeply himself, he smelled sex, exotic and compelling. Both masculine and feminine shades of lust combined within the scent and drove him mad.

There was no time left. As much as he would've liked to go on forever, when she rubbed her hips to his again, he was undone.

He belted his arm around her waist and pulled her hard against him, thrusting again. The next few moments whizzed by in a blur of thrusts—deeper, deeper, again and again.

Higher and higher, lost and crazed, his muscles tensed and strained as he fought to hold on. He heard her scream, then curse something unintelligible as she twisted and lurched. She plastered herself to him, seeming to want the melding of the two of them into one entity.

That was all he needed. His climax surged through him like an earthquake. His whole body shook with the force. He braced his trembling legs and went along for the ride.

Bending nearly in two, he brought his mouth down on her neck, nipping and grazing and loving the sweetness and softness of her. One last thrust and his head came up as he gasped for breath.

Talk about your life-changing experiences.

He picked her up in his arms and headed for the bed. All he wanted now was another few hours. *Or* maybe, a whole lifetime of feeling this damned good.

Chapter 13

Rosie stretched out beside Jericho's sleeping body. Only moments before he'd laid her down on the bed and crawled in after her. Feeling limp and sated, she was amazed that her body still pulsed with pleasure. Surely there had never been anything in her previous life to compare to him and the things they'd done.

From that very first moment when he'd echoed her thoughts and said he hoped they never uncovered her past, she'd been all his. Forever. Whatever he wanted. For however long he wanted.

Still, at the beginning she'd felt compelled to tell him she loved him. That he was the only one there would ever be from this moment on. It had seemed so important to say the actual words. But quickly she'd come to the conclusion that words didn't matter.

He'd been such a master at telling her everything he was feeling without words. She'd felt his need throbbing inside her. She'd known his thoughts, begging her to never leave him as he'd worked hard to make sure she was fulfilled before taking his own pleasure.

For this short time with him, she'd forgotten all about her fears and the tension of having people after her. And now she wanted to find a way of forgetting them for good. To let Jericho become her permanent protector, so that together they could conquer all the bad things in the world.

He wanted that, too. She was positive. But just now she lay quietly racking her brain for the best way of communicating their mutual needs.

When he softly snored, she found the sounds of him beside her, seemingly so comfortable and sated himself, terribly endearing. He'd been through so much for her. He needed a little sleep.

Easing out from under his arm, she inched away and stood, turning back to look at him on the bed. So beautiful. She vaguely knew that wasn't how you were supposed to describe a man, especially a tough guy like this one. But she thought Jericho was simply gorgeous.

The strong chin. The hint of stubble. Those long lashes lying against the high curve of his cheek.

Whew. Despite the cool air-conditioning in the room, a trickle of sweat beaded at her temple and slithered down her neck. Rosie walked to the bathroom, found a glass and drank water, trying to cool off.

But knowing he was there on the bed, naked, brought her back to the doorway so she could stare at him some more. Just to look at those broad shoulders that had been absolutely perfect to hold on to during the throes of passion. They narrowed down to lean hips. And it was all sleek, flat muscle in between.

Half the time she thought he was some kind of throwback to the old West. The strong, silent type. But when they were alone together, his eyes told her something entirely different as they changed colors with his moods.

Granite when he was mad or taking his job seriously. Amber when he was being sincere or teaching her how to shoot. And almost jade-green when he was in the midst of giving her passion. That last image, the one of him gazing intently into her eyes with those fantastic green eyes, made her actually shiver as the heated desire skittered down her spine.

How could she explain that she wanted forever from him without scaring him or turning him off?

He stirred, rolling onto his back. The sight of all that manhood moved her to action. Thinking simply stopped.

She slid into the bed beside him, tempted beyond restraint. Taking him into her hands, she stroked and played and massaged. First she ran a forefinger down one long, smooth side. Next a tender touch to the rounded, slick tip.

When his body began to respond to her ministrations, she leaned in and took him into her mouth. A soft groan came from above her but what she was doing felt so indulgent, so right, that she refused to give it up.

Jericho came awake with a jolt of erotic sensation. When he looked down at the top of Rosie's head and realized what she was doing to him, he reached out for her. But she shied away from his hands.

Sweet mercy. The vibrations alone nearly caused him to come three feet off the bed.

Very much more of that and it would be all over. And though one day that might be a good plan to follow, it wasn't what he had in mind for tonight.

He wanted tonight to be all about her pleasure. Needing to make her see how much she meant to him. Desperate to make her understand that he did want her to stay with him forever. Tonight was supposed to be hers.

Tunneling his hands through her hair, he firmly eased her back. She lifted her head and looked at him and the sight of her glazed eyes and satisfied expression was a bigger turn-on than what she'd been doing.

Rock hard, he moved fast. Twisting their bodies with a roll and a plunge, he found himself inside her again. Right where he wanted to be.

Her body was slick with sweat but so was his. A momentary thought of moving this show into the shower came and went. Later. The next time. And there would be more. Lots more. Until both of them were weak and weeping and had no more questions about a future.

He eased out of her and then back inside again with a slow draw, setting up a rhythm he hoped to continue for a good long while. Hot damn but this was heaven.

She rocked hard against his hips, sending another blast of pure pleasure spinning through his veins. He reached down and cupped her bottom, holding her tightly to him.

Their bodies were on fire everywhere they touched. So damned hot he figured they might combust.

"Jericho, you feel so good."

"Back attcha, darlin'." *Good* didn't seem adequate. But so help him, his brain must be melting. Words were impossible.

He leaned down and kissed her, moving in and out and loving the feel of silky wet heat. Hoping somehow to make her see.

But he wasn't exactly positive about everything he wanted her to know. Except that he needed her to stay. Was that enough?

"I love you," she said on a moan as her body began tightening around him.

He thrust again on a long slow glide. Was this really what love felt like? Was that what he needed to say?

But before his mouth could catch up, she arched her back and her whole body went rigid. "Jericho!"

Nature took over then, freeing him from thinking, as his own movements came faster and faster. Pounding hard into her, too soon the orgasm broke through him on a flood of flashing sensation. He barked out a unintelligible curse and went with the flow.

Collapsing beside her afterward, he rolled them until he had her captured in his embrace and spooned against his chest. He lay there for a few seconds, smiling into the back of her head.

He breathed in the smell of her shampoo, and thought it might be the nicest scent ever invented. Not sure if it was some kind of flower or just the smell of clean, he figured he could certainly get used to it.

Running a hand along the smooth skin of her arm and amazing himself by becoming hard again so soon, Jericho figured he could certainly get used to this part, too. They were sure good together. Idly he wondered if they had the stamina to keep it up all night.

Then Rosie moaned, turning in his arms and moving in close. He felt her breath, hot along his neck. Her breasts pressed tight and hard against his chest. And without question he knew there was one thing for certain.

He had all the strength he needed for this night.

Rosie leaned back against the bed's headboard, a silly grin plastered across her face, and listened as Jericho shaved and finished getting dressed in the bathroom. What a wonderful night it had been. She didn't know if she'd ever had one quite like it before, but it didn't matter. Not now that she was sure she would be spending many more nights in the same way.

Well, that is if she could hold up. She probably hadn't gotten more than an hour's worth of sleep during the whole night. But at the moment she couldn't possibly feel any better even if she'd slept for days. She wasn't sick to her stomach and it was midmorning already. Maybe sex was good for that too.

She was in love. And though Jericho hadn't said it in so many words—that he loved her and wanted her to spend the rest of her life with him—he'd made his feelings perfectly clear in all the things he'd done and the ways he had treated her.

Hmm. *Mrs. Jericho Yates.* That seemed as good a name as any for her to take. In fact, a lot better than most.

Thinking about her missing name brought up a subject she would rather not consider. Her past. But more than her past, who was chasing her and why. Had she stolen something? If only she could remember.

She thought back to the one and only breakthrough to her past that her mind had yielded—the dream of a prince turning into a monster. The prince from her nightmare had looked a little like Sheriff Montalvo, only taller and much more sophisticated and suave.

Sheriff Montalvo. Her skin crawled just at the thought of him. Now *there* was someone to worry about. Rosie wondered what he was doing this morning. Had Jericho's friend, the sheriff from this county, contacted Montalvo about the attack and crash already?

Curious, she picked up a remote from the bedside table and turned on the television that was housed in a beautiful antique armoire across the room. Maybe there would be some news about the missing men. Flipping through the channels, trying to find a local station, Rosie caught the tail end of an image that stopped her cold.

Her mouth sagged open as she backed up the channels until the picture came onto the screen once again. Then all of a sudden, there he was. Her nightmare prince.

No mistaking him. The tall regal bearing. The dark brown hair combed in an impeccable style. Conveniently, the fellow was even wearing a tux. Whoever the man on the TV screen was turned then and gave the camera a generous smile. A deep dimple on his left cheek was all it took to make some things click into place for Rosie.

The man she was staring at, her nightmare prince, was also most definitely her baby's father. And there he was, live and in color, right on the television. Oh. My. God.

* * *

Jericho turned off the water and folded his towel. From behind his back he heard the TV running. Rosie must've turned it on while she was waiting for him to finish getting dressed.

The fleeting thought of her caused his lips to spread into another of the big, stupid grins that he'd been plagued with all morning. She was perfect. He could barely wait to begin their lives together. He wanted lots more nights. Lots more time to find ways of telling her how much he cared.

But not until after they got a few other things taken care of today. He needed to borrow a truck to get them back to Esperanza, and he wanted to go long before dark. His friend Sam had called a while ago to say Sheriff Montalvo had taken over the crews searching for crash victims in the arroyo. After all, the scene was located in his county.

But that knowledge did nothing to calm Jericho's nerves. He was positive Montalvo had had something to do with those men in the first place. And he didn't like knowing a man as powerful as a sheriff might be after Rosie.

Rosie. Another smile crossed his lips. One thing he needed to do today was tell her how much he wanted her in his life for good. Maybe while they were driving back to Esperanza would be as good a time as any.

He picked up his clean shirt, freshly laundered courtesy of the staff of the bed-and-breakfast, and shoved his arms into the sleeves. As he buttoned down, he tuned into what was happening on the television behind his back. It sounded like a news story. Had Rosie found a story about the attack and crash?

Turning and taking the few steps out into the bedroom, Jericho was shocked with what he saw. Rosie sat hypnotized by something she was watching on the screen. He glanced at it but didn't see anything exciting. It was nothing but a national news story about the presidential candidates. Still, Rosie's face had gone pale. Her eyes were glazed and her mouth hung open. She seemed paralyzed. Completely lost in something on the screen.

"What's the matter?" he asked as he moved to her side. "Is everything okay?"

No reply.

"Are you okay, darlin'?" He took her by the shoulders and gently forced her to face him.

He could see her fighting to bring his features into focus. Her features were contorted with fear. What on earth could be the matter?

"Rosie. Honey. Talk to me."

"It's him. I...I mean... It's starting to come back." She grabbed for his hand and he captured both of hers. They were ice-cold.

"What's coming back?"

"Jericho, look." She pointed at the television screen but all he saw there was the Texas governor, giving what seemed to be an ordinary political campaign speech for his run for the presidency of the United States.

"Governor Daniels?"

"Allan Daniels. Yes. That's him. That's my baby's father. I'm positive."

Worried about her growing hysterical state, Jericho

sat at the edge of the bed and gathered her close. "Calm down, sweetheart. I know you may think this is real, but it doesn't seem possible. Allan Daniels? How? Why?"

"I don't know." She frowned and knitted her eyebrows. "I can't remember any of that. My own name isn't even coming back. But I know this for sure. Allan Daniels is the man I was with. The only man. I know it."

Standing in tall grass at an isolated bend in the Rio Grande River, Arnie watched in the distance as a marked sheriff's SUV drove down the dusty side road, heading for the clearing. Montalvo. It was about time.

Glad his bleeding had stopped some time ago, Arnie fingered the cut across his cheek. Damn it. The thing would probably leave a deep scar.

Arnie needed help to cross the border so he could find medical assistance, and Montalvo was going to provide that help. The *boss* had said the sheriff would do what he could. And what the boss said, happened.

After all, it was Montalvo's brilliant idea that had gotten him into the big mess last night. What the hell had Arnie, a big-city guy, known about the range land after dark? Or of that arroyo area. Or of stupid dumb-ass cows for that matter.

Nothing. Zip. But he did know how to climb out of a busted SUV and scramble up the side of a brush-strewn arroyo to save his butt. And he also knew enough to drag the driver's dead body free and hide it good.

Most of all, Arnie had known to call the boss and beg for forgiveness and help. After all, there was no one else on earth who could help him if the boss refused.

The sheriff's SUV pulled into the clearing and stopped, the engine still running. A blacked-out side window rolled down and Montalvo stared at him from behind huge aviator sunglasses.

"It's about time," Arnie said. "I've been waiting."

"Shut up."

A chill rode up Arnie's spine and he secretly fingered the .45 hidden under his shirt. This was not going down well. Montalvo was always a snake anyway.

"Did the boss tell you what I need?" Arnie tried once more to be heard. "I just want an easy way across the river without the U.S. Border Patrol shooting me on sight. Nothing else. I swear."

"I know what your boss wants," Montalvo said menacingly and reached down as if for a weapon.

Uh-oh.

To hell with it. Arnie palmed his gun and fired point-blank exactly at the moment he twisted and headed for the river, going at a dead run.

Only thirty or forty feet from the steep riverbank to start, he knew he could make it in a few seconds if he wasn't shot dead before getting there.

For those few seconds nothing happened behind him. No sounds or shouting. No lights from Border Patrol units. Maybe he was home free. Maybe he'd plugged Montalvo. And maybe Montalvo had agreed to meet here because he knew this place had a gap in the Border Patrol area. Maybe.

That son of a bitch Montalvo. He'd meant to kill him.

If Arnie hadn't actually finished Montalvo with his lucky shot, he vowed to come back and do the job right. After he found safety in Mexico, of course.

Arnie hit the river running and never stopped. Splashing across the two-foot-deep water, it occurred to him belatedly that Montalvo would never have had the nerve to ambush him if the boss hadn't agreed. Hell. If the boss wanted him dead, he might as well stop breathing.

At the Mexican side of the river, Arnie took a huge breath and figured he had a few more hours to live. He would try to figure out something.

But then he looked up the bank and spotted a whole squad of Mexican *federales* staring down at him. Or at least they looked like they were part of the Mexican army.

Until…they pointed their AK-47s in his direction and began firing.

Chapter 14

"So what'd you do to her, man?" Clay Colton stood on his own front step with his hands on his hips, scowling down at Jericho.

Clay might be his best bud, and he'd been nice enough to let Rosie stay here at his ranch again last night. But Jericho would be damned if he would let Clay interrogate him. He stuck his hands in his pockets and looked away.

"It's none of your business," Jericho said through gritted teeth. "Is she ready to go?"

"Tamara is with her. Apparently she cried all night and has been sick to her stomach all morning. So what happened? Where are you two going today? 'Cause I heard her tell Tamara that she didn't want to go."

Yesterday Jericho had heard all Rosie's reasons for not wanting to go to Austin and confront the governor. But he was just as determined to show up for their appointment with Allan Daniels as ever. She was the one who'd insisted Daniels was her lover, after all.

Jericho would never forget it. Not if he lived to be a hundred. After their fantastic night, and just as he was trying to find a way to tell her he wanted her to be his forever. That's when she'd burst out with the news.

In so many words, she'd said, "Oh, by the way, thanks for saving my life and for one really great night. But I see my old life on the TV. And there's no way for you to live up to its sophistication and power."

Hell.

From that moment on they'd disagreed about calling the governor and arranging a meeting. But though it had taken him all afternoon and most of the night, Jericho had been determined that Rosie needed to confront her past—if Daniels really was that past.

He'd finally done it, too. Found an assistant to an assistant who agreed to get Rosie a moment with the governor. Between Daniels's regular duties and his busy campaign schedule, it had not been easy. And for the whole time, Rosie had begged him not to make her go.

Jericho didn't understand her. If she really was happy here with him, as she said, why bring up her past at all? He'd come to the conclusion that she wasn't happy and contented here. Either Daniels was her child's father and deserved to know about it. Or he wasn't and Rosie had invented the whole Daniels thing to ease out of a relationship with Jericho that had grown pretty intense.

Eventually, early last evening, he'd brought her out here to stay with Clay and Tamara for the night and then spent his own night brooding at home.

"Well?" Clay was waiting for some kind of answer.

"We're driving to Austin to check on a lead to her past. I don't know why she's saying she doesn't want to go."

"Maybe she's scared," Clay offered. "She's been kidnapped and shot at a couple of times. I know that would give me more than a moment's pause about driving around the countryside with you."

Jericho frowned again. "Thanks for the vote of confidence. But I think she might be okay from now on.

"Last night Sheriff Montalvo in San Javier County was found shot to death in his official sheriff's unit, parked down by the Rio Grande. They also found the body of a known hitman nearby in the river. The theory is that it was some kind of Mexican drug deal gone sour."

"Montalvo? Rosie said something about how creepy he seemed and that maybe he was behind the attack against you down by Gage's Arroyo the night before last."

Jericho nodded and heaved a sigh. "Yeah. I've come to the conclusion Rosie must've been somehow involved with Montalvo in her past. And that he was the one who hired those goons to come after her.

"I intend to keep investigating what his motives might've been and what precipitated the kidnapping. But with Montalvo dead, I think she should be okay."

He figured maybe she would be *more* okay with her old life rather than with him in a new one. At least she wouldn't have to keep looking over her shoulder. She could relax and heal. And while he worked to get over her and figure it all out, he wouldn't have to keep worrying about saving her life.

Twisting her hands together nervously, Rosie peered down the hall as they stepped out of the elevator. They were on the sixth floor of the Austin office building that supposedly housed the governor's campaign head-quarters. She really didn't want to be here. But Jericho had insisted.

She still couldn't figure out what had gone so suddenly wrong with him. All during their fabulous and intimate night, Jericho had given her everything. He'd made her every wish come true. She'd been so positive the rest of their lives would stay that way.

But right after she'd had the vision of her and Daniels, um, making a baby, Jericho had changed into someone else entirely. Someone angry and withdrawn.

He'd barely said a word to her since then. His attitude had surprised the devil out of her. After all, he had to have known *someone* else was the baby's father. But he'd suddenly started insisting they go to Austin and confront the governor rather than talk it over, figure out the truth and learn why no one had reported her missing.

Rosie wasn't too sure why she didn't want to see Daniels. But maybe it was for just that very reason. Why hadn't he cared enough to report her absence? Why weren't the Texas Rangers and all the county sheriffs out looking for her? He was the governor. He had the power to find her anywhere, if he wanted to.

She took a couple of steps along the rather ordinary-looking hallway behind Jericho and hesitated. Yes, this place did seem vaguely familiar. But it also seemed scary. She didn't like it.

"What's the matter? Come on." Jericho turned, and she wished she could see his eyes better but they were hidden under his broad-brimmed sheriff's Stetson. He took her by the elbow and gently tugged her forward. "We just barely managed to get this appointment. We can't be late for it."

"I don't…" She was shaking so badly that she couldn't speak. What if she'd been wrong and Daniels didn't even recognize her? They shouldn't be here. Everything just felt bad.

But right then Jericho stopped in front of the door marked as the Daniels's campaign headquarters. He opened it and drew her inside with him.

A couple of women stood at a reception desk. Both of them were engrossed in something on the desktop and didn't glance up. Directly behind them was a big open room with rows of long tables, all empty at the moment. Off to each side were a couple of office spaces with closed doors. Everything had a temporary and bare feeling.

Both of the women were dressed in pantsuits, very businesslike. One was in her twenties, blond and pretty. The other must've been in her fifties. She had salt-and-pepper gray hair, but it was cut with sophistication and made her face look fragile. Jericho cleared his throat to get the women's attention.

The older one looked up first. "Olivia! You're back. It seems like you've been out forever. How're you feeling? Are you finally completely well?"

Olivia? Rosie took a step backward, but Jericho held tight to her arm and kept her beside him.

The second woman had lifted her head by then. "What on earth did you do to your hair?" She tilted her chin to study Rosie. "I simply loved all your long blond hair, Olivia. It always made me so jealous. This style isn't too terrible, though…I guess. It frames your face. But the color. Why in heaven's name did you darken it? That shade doesn't do a thing for you."

Jericho moved forward a few feet, dragging her along. Rosie's feet didn't move willingly. In fact, her whole body was going numb. These women weren't the least bit familiar to her, even though they seemed to know her well.

"You know this woman?" Jericho asked them.

They both looked at him as though he had materialized out of the woodwork.

The older one recovered first. "Of course we do, Sheriff…uh…Sheriff…"

"Yates. Sheriff Jericho Yates from Campo County. I called about an appointment with Governor Daniels for our amnesia victim."

"Amnesia? Our Olivia? Really?" The older woman stared into Rosie's eyes.

"Then you do know her," he interjected, taking charge of the situation, as he usually did. "How? What's her full name?"

"Olivia Halprin," the younger of the two blurted out and then also came closer to study Rosie. "And we work with her. She's Governor Daniels's campaign treasurer. She's been out sick with the flu for the last ten days.

"Or at least that's what we all thought," she amended.

Rosie's knees were trembling and she was afraid she

might be sick again. Clinging to Jericho's arm, she fought to bring images to her mind. Any images.

The name *Olivia* did sort of ring a bell. Maybe Olivia was her real name. At least it could be. But that was all there was. Nothing else was making any sense.

One of the two side doors opened and Allan Daniels stuck his head out. "What's going on out here?" He turned to her and his eyes widened. "Olivia. Sweetheart. There you are. How are you feeling? Better, I hope."

A picture formed in Rosie's head of kissing those smiling lips. Of kissing the nightmare prince.

With legs collapsing under her, she started down a long dark tunnel. Where things began growing smaller and smaller, like *Alice in Wonderland,* until her whole world simply disappeared.

Sometime later Rosie lay back on the leather couch in Allan's office with her eyes closed and listening to Jericho finish explaining to Allan how he'd found her and about everything they'd been through for the last few days.

It all sounded fantastic. But to her it was the only reality. She still couldn't come to grips with an old life. A few shadows, like old black-and-white movies moved across her consciousness. But most of it didn't stick around long enough for her to bring it into focus.

Shifting a plastic baggie full of ice that one of the women had plopped on her forehead after she'd been carried to this couch, she remained quiet with her eyes closed. But she still paid attention as the two men talked about her as if she were someone else.

"I can't believe she's been through all that just in the

time she's been gone," Allan said. "We were lucky you were the one who found her, Jericho. You don't mind me calling you that, do you? I owe you a big debt of gratitude and I hope to find a way to pay you back."

Allan hesitated and Rosie could just picture him taking off his jacket and loosening his tie, the big phony. "So you believe this Sheriff Montalvo from San Javier County was somehow responsible for the things that happened to Olivia?" The image of Allan Daniels was now firmly formed in her mind. From her past. And from her present.

Jericho must've nodded his head because she didn't hear him agree. She might not be able to see him, but she was tuned into his responses. Feeling him growing colder, more distant, with every passing moment, she wished they could leave. She couldn't really blame Jericho. With every word and movement Allan seemed more snakelike and slimy. How could she have ever let herself be conned by the man?

"Well, then," Allan said to Jericho. "I would take it as a personal favor if you'd follow up on that. I'll put you in touch with Chief Aldeen of the Rangers. He'll see you get all the help you need for your investigation."

"Thank you, sir."

"You're…"

"Allan." Rosie decided it was time to come back into this life, though truthfully she was as hesitant as Jericho. Most of the things that belonged in her previous world were still only vague images. And not all of them would apparently be full of sunshine and light. There continued to be lots of dark, black holes that she couldn't— or wouldn't—fill in.

And all of it seemed to circle around the governor of Texas, for crying out loud.

"Olivia, you're up," Allan said as he came close and helped her to stand. "Are you sure you don't need to be checked out at a hospital?"

"No," she heard herself say. "A doctor looked me over in Esperanza. I'm going to be fine."

He gave her an odd look, and Rosie wondered if he had any idea she was pregnant. She would bet not. Well, it remained to be seen whether she ever told him the truth. At the moment, chances were slim.

Like a silent beacon of hope, Rosie felt drawn instead toward Jericho, who stood behind the desk. He was her savior. Her protector. Her love.

Shooting her a rather creepy and lecherous look, Allan let his gaze linger on her breasts. Her growing unease around him became an urgent sense that she needed to get out of here. Away from this man.

Allan put his arm around her shoulders, and a disgusted shudder skittered clear down her spine. Why was she so sure this guy was not who he seemed? She inched away without making a big deal.

"I just want to go home." Amazingly, she did remember where her old condo was all of a sudden. However, she found herself dearly wishing to go to the *home* a hundred miles southwest in a blip on the map called Esperanza.

Allan's pleasant expression turned frustrated. "I can't take you home right now. I have that $10,000-a-plate fund-raiser coming up in a couple of hours. You remember—you set it up."

She did not remember. Nor did she want to. It was all wrong. Wrong. Wrong.

Afraid Allan might insist she go with him, she began, "I can get there by…"

"I'll see her safely home, sir." Jericho had moved to stand at attention by the door, but he interrupted her firmly and came closer. "If you'll give me her address, I'd be happy to take care of it."

Jericho sounded like a damned bodyguard. Was that all their time together meant to him? Just because she was on the governor's campaign staff and probably had sex with the man—

"That would be terrific, Jericho, if you wouldn't mind," Allan said in what she vaguely remembered were his normal, charming tones. Then he turned to her. "There's always been a spare set of keys to both your condo and your car stashed in your office. Just in case of emergencies. Let's go see if they're still there. Then all of us can be on our way. And I'll contact you later at home."

"I wonder what happened to my car?" Rosie said absently as Jericho unlocked her condo and ushered the two of them inside.

She lived on the twelfth floor of a downtown building with parking below and a doorman in residence. Jericho wasn't surprised at the condo's sweeping views of Austin and the Hill Country from the floor-to-ceiling windows.

"You don't remember?" he asked as he hesitated just inside the threshold. "What kind of car do you own?"

"A Mercedes S550." After a silent instant, she continued with a grin. "Wow. A few minutes ago I couldn't have come up with that answer. Things are just flashing into my brain at lightning speed."

She strolled wide-eyed through the large foyer and stepped into the sunken living room. Gracefully, she walked around the room, touching white leather couches, staring at expensive artwork on the walls, marveling at marble sculptures. The furnishings seemed to bring memories back into her mind.

Jericho wasn't too pleased to see this much opulence. No expert, he still would bet there was several hundred thousand dollars' worth of art and sculptures skillfully placed around the room. And her car was a Mercedes. Of course it was. Daniels no doubt kept his girlfriend in diamonds, too.

How could his handmade cabin and seven-year-old truck ever compete with all this? How could he ever hope to compete with the *governor of Texas?*

The answer was simple, he couldn't.

But he could do his job and also do the governor his favor at the same time. "If you'll give me your license number and a description, I'll report your car as missing. We'll find it."

She nodded idly. "Thanks."

"Are more things coming back?" he asked, hoping against hope that they weren't. That she would only ever remember him and their time together. He had to guess it was already too late for that.

"A few," she told him. "Like the fact that my birth name is Olivia DeVille Halprin. The only child of Chester Halprin and Suzanne DeVille. And before he passed away, my father built an Internet empire that's been valued in the billions."

Oh? Maybe it wasn't Daniels's money that had provided all the opulence then. But that didn't give Jericho much comfort. He still couldn't live up to any of this. Never would.

"So your father is no longer alive. How about your mother? I'm wondering why she didn't report you missing?"

Rosie turned and graced him with a wry smile. "As cold and ruthless as my father was, Suzanne is just the opposite. Beautiful and outgoing and a pillar in hundreds of Texas charitable foundations. She has just never had much time for a daughter. She's much too busy devoting her life to really good causes.

"I haven't talked to my mother in months." Rosie continued a little too quietly. "In almost a year now, I think. But I'm sure she would've missed me eventually."

Jericho couldn't imagine such a family. Okay, so his mother had disappeared and never come back. But both his father and his brother had always been the rocks in his life. What would he have become without his family?

He took a step in Rosie's…no Olivia's…direction before coming up short. He didn't know Olivia Halprin, and he had absolutely nothing in common with her. She wouldn't want sympathy from him, and he couldn't stand to have her back out of his arms when she realized the same thing.

Olivia blinked a couple of times then said, "A *bath?*"

"Excuse me?" He hadn't said anything about a bath. She shook her head as though to clear it. "What? Oh, sorry. I don't know why I said that. I never take baths. But it just popped into my head while I was thinking that things seem a little off."

"A little off? How do you mean?"

Shrugging, she turned and walked over to open one of the many doors that led off the main room. "My office is in here. Let me see if it feels funny, too."

Jericho shoved his hands in his pockets and followed. Funny feelings were not in his jurisdiction.

Olivia's office was crammed with computer equipment. It made him wonder if she'd inherited her father's genius.

"Before I became the Daniels campaign treasurer," she began as she studied the machines up close, "I was a CPA. A Certified Public Accountant. That's just what I love to do. I know it doesn't sound interesting, but I specialized in forensic accounting. Chasing bad guys around inside their bank accounts."

She turned and smiled at him. A real smile. "Maybe that's why I fell under the spell of a lawman. You think?"

He couldn't talk to her about that right now, so he shrugged one shoulder and stayed quiet.

Her smile faded slowly, then she turned and moved one of the keyboards a few inches to the left. "I swear it feels like someone has been in here since I was last in this room. I'm sort of fussy—okay *anal* would be a better word—about my workspace. Everything has to be just so. Must be the accountant in me.

"And my things have been moved. I could swear to it."

"You sure it isn't just that it's been a while?" he asked soothingly. "Your security alarm was still armed when we came in. We had to disarm it. Besides, you've been through a lot over the last few days. Especially with your memory. Maybe things are still hazy in your mind."

She looked around. "Lots of things are still a little hazy. But not this room." Sighing, she turned back to him. "I guess I need more time. How long are we going to stay here? Do I have time for a bath?"

Those seemed like odd questions, but he decided it was past time for him to get out of town. Let her have her bath and anything else she needed. The lady was home. She hardly needed him to stick around anymore, despite the fact that leaving was bound to kill him.

"You go on and take your bath. I've got to be heading back to Esperanza. Just come see me to the door. Make sure your doors are locked and the security alarm is set behind me."

"You're leaving without me? But…"

"Look, *Olivia*. You're where you belong. You have a job and people who care about you. But I sure don't belong here. Let's just cut our losses while we still can."

Her face crumbled and big tears welled in her eyes.

"I'll stay in touch," he offered. "Let you know how the investigation is coming along. And I'll be sure to work on finding your car."

She sniffed and reached out a hand to him. "But can't you see that I don't belong here anymore, either? No one in my old life even bothered to check up on me. That would never happen in Esperanza. I need…"

Jericho needed to get out of there—fast. "You'll change your mind when more things start coming back. I mean, for one, yours would be the only Mercedes in all of Esperanza, Texas. And that's just for starters. There's no place to shop. We don't have any art museums. I can't think of anybody who would need the services of a CPA."

He waved his hand as if that explained everything. And to him, it did. He could never stand to work at making a life with her only to lose her back to the big city.

The worst had happened. She was regaining her memory and that meant he wouldn't stand a chance in the long run. Just like his mother, only for different reasons, she'd be off and running before he could turn around.

"Lock up behind me," he said as he turned tail and made a dash for the door. "I'll contact you."

Maybe. *If* his heart could stand the pain of hearing her voice and knowing his house would forever stand barren and lonely without her there.

Damn her all to hell for making him believe it could happen. Believe he could get what he wanted for once.

Well, Sheriff Jericho Yates would be just fine alone.

Chapter 15

Furious at herself for being such a hormone-raging wimp, Rosie slashed at the tears streaming down her cheeks. She'd finished locking up behind the retreating Jericho, and then had come to the conclusion that she might as well have that bath, so that's where she was headed.

How could he have left her here in Austin all alone?

She *should've* said he had to take her with him. That his job wasn't done and they hadn't even had a chance to talk. She *should've* said something about her things being still in his closet and that at the least she needed to say goodbye to the dogs. She *should've* grabbed him and kissed him senseless, just to remind him of everything they'd done together.

But she'd been so surprised, so thrown by the idea

of how shallow her old life had been, that she hadn't thought fast enough to get out a word. All the should'ves in the world didn't matter when the person you counted on turned his back on you and walked away.

In her old life it had been easy to blame her distant, cold father for all her unhappiness. But in truth, she remembered now how it really was. She'd tried desperately hard to become the most beautiful and successful daughter a father could ever want. No matter what she did, though, he'd never seen her efforts—not really. So to emulate her father, make him see her, she'd learned to appreciate art, as he had, and forced herself to like the other superficial things in life that meant a lot to him. But of course, *her* list of superficial things also ended up including dating gorgeous, powerful and successful men with no scruples.

That was how she'd been drawn to Allan Daniels in the first place. But giving up her old job to please him had been the craziest part. The only thing in her life that she'd ever done that made any real sense was to work at the forensic accounting consulting firm. She'd tossed it all the minute Allan crooked his little finger at her.

Rosie turned on the bath water and thought of Jericho— not Allan. Thought of how much better her life had been with the Campo County sheriff. In just a few short days, she'd turned herself into someone who could be appreciated and respected. Because of him. He had really taken time to see her for herself. Not for only the outside.

But stupid her, she'd just let him walk away.

Sitting on the edge of the filling tub, Rosie hung her head and wept for all the things she had not done or said that might've made a difference. Might've made Jericho wait for her. Want her.

This place—this life—weren't hers anymore. So she would refuse to stay here, by heaven. After she took this bath and rested a little, she would rent a car and drive right back to Esperanza, Texas. Back where she belonged.

An odd, instant and intense urge to put bath salts into the water had her reaching for the fancy jar she'd never opened but only used for decoration. Though once she had the clear bottle in hand, she *knew.* In her mind she could actually see herself hiding something deep inside the fuchsia crystals.

Standing up beside the vanity, Rosie dumped the contents of the salt jar out on the counter. The clunk of something hard and metallic captured her attention. What had she hidden? And why?

In another moment, at least the *what* was clear. Out of the baths crystals rolled a tiny flash drive. Hmm.

Fighting to remember more, she turned off the bath water and headed to her office. It should be easy enough to find out the *why* by plugging the drive into one of her computers.

The curiosity was killing her.

Cut and run! He'd done it again.

Jericho eased on the brakes of his borrowed SUV and pulled into a roadside park off the 290 that was not quite in Johnson City. A half hour out of Austin and he was finally getting his head on straight. About damned time.

With the engine idling, he beat his fists against the steering wheel and wondered what the hell was the matter with him. In his whole life, every time a woman got too close, he would shut down and split. That was just who he was. Call it pride. Call it not wanting to take a chance on being hurt. Whatever. But never before had it seemed this important, or this wrong to run.

All those other times the women were perfectly fine, and maybe he could've made a life with them. But this time. This time it was Rosie and she was…she was…

Everything.

Jericho drew a deep breath and tried to think instead of letting his emotions tie him up in knots. Why was he always like this, shutting down without a fight? Could he change this time? After all, he never backed down from other challenges in his life.

But with that thought in his mind, a picture of Allan Daniels leering at Rosie with a malevolent gleam in his eye and yet another picture of Rosie begging him not to take her there, made him rethink all that had taken place.

There were several missing pieces to the puzzle of Rosie. Big missing pieces. Like, what had those goons wanted from her? *It.* They'd kept mentioning an *it.* Was Rosie going to suddenly remember what that was and then be in terrible danger again?

Jericho had walked off the job before it was done. He had never done that in his life.

Putting the SUV in gear, he prepared to turn around. Had he been so intimidated by Daniels's position as governor that he'd lost his mind? There was nothing right about the whole scenario. If Rosie and Daniels had been such great lovers, then why hadn't Daniels gone to her condo to check on her when he'd thought she was sick? He knew if she'd been *his* girlfriend and had really been sick with the flu, Jericho would've stuck to her bedside like glue.

Who the heck had reported that she had the flu in the first place?

Lots of problems. Lots of big red flags that should've caught his attention.

But the worst of it was that he hadn't listened to Rosie. He hadn't given her a chance to talk. She had become his whole world and he'd turned his back? Stupid. Stupid.

Pulling out onto 290, he stepped on the gas and retraced his route back to Austin. Back to Rosie. Maybe she would give him a second chance. Maybe he could make her see that he was willing to fight to save her—fight to love her.

He just hoped to hell it wasn't too late.

Rosie sat staring at the monitor, too stunned to move. Everything—all the secrets and terrible truths—came back in a rush of clarity.

Allan Daniels was dirty. More, Allan was an embezzler who consorted with Mexican druglords—and he was running for president of the United States. Holy moly.

She remembered well her first instance of finding these horrible facts on an innocuous-looking flash drive in Allan's office. Almost ten days ago now. After convincing herself of the reality of what she was seeing, she'd been nearly hysterical wondering what she should do next. Who to go to who would not only believe her but who could do something to stop him.

The governor of Texas was the head of the Texas Rangers. So that was out. The police? The FBI? She remembered thinking they might laugh at her—or worse—ignore her. He was, after all, a candidate for the presidency, and everyone figured all his secrets were already out.

Not by half.

After taking the precautionary step of hiding the flash drive in her bath salts and making a copy to hide in her car, she'd done the only other thing that made sense. She'd contacted an old friend, a reporter for the *Dallas Morning News,* who was honest and who could start a secret investigation that could eventually bring Allan down.

Mary Beth Caldwell. My God. What had happened to her?

Rosie remembered their secret meeting at Stubbins Barbeque. Remembered distinctly sitting across from Mary Beth, who looked a lot like Becky French, in her early sixties, short and plump. But Mary Beth was a shark. Smart and well-connected, as an investigative reporter she could not be beat.

Mary Beth had not only believed her about Allan, but had agreed to hide Rosie until the authorities could be convinced. Rosie had already realized she was in dire trouble because Allan had called her cell while she was with Mary Beth. He'd wanted to know if she'd seen anyone strange near his office. Obviously, he'd already missed his flash drive and knew she was the only one who could've taken it.

She and Mary Beth had immediately left the barbeque joint and headed for Rosie's car. But before they got there, a couple of dangerous-looking men came up behind them. Rosie remembered running, then a thud coming from behind her. Mary Beth must've been hit, but she'd been too afraid to turn back to help. Oh, God. Rosie's stomach clinched.

She remembered dropping her car keys and running. Running for her life and not looking back. A trucker had picked her up down the highway, and she'd thought she might be okay if she got far enough away. When that good-guy driver dropped her off in Rio View, Rosie had done the smart thing and headed straight to the sheriff for help. Sheriff Montalvo.

Yeah, Montalvo had helped all right. He'd helped her find a motel to hide in. And then he'd apparently called the governor to help himself to whatever clandestine reward Allan must've been offering for her.

Now Montalvo was dead. Mary Beth was probably dead. With sudden clear panic, she knew she was as good as dead, too.

Oh, Jericho, where are you? She reached for the phone to call him at the exact moment when she heard a slight noise in another part of the condo. Not much of a noise. But enough to keep her from being surprised as the voice she'd dreaded to hear came from directly behind her back.

"Put the phone down, Olivia."

She did as he demanded and slowly turned to face what looked like a silencer attached to a huge gun. "Hello, Allan," she managed without looking at his face. "I thought you were at that fund-raiser. Where's your secret-service security detail?"

Oh, hell, she was done. She hadn't remembered enough of her past in time. With just a few more minutes, she could've been out the door and gone. Of course now that it didn't help her, she remembered that Allan had access to a duplicate key and knew her security codes. That was the very last thing she'd remembered and probably the last thought she would ever have.

He chuckled. "Yeah, I gave them all the slip. The secret service thinks I'm having a quickie fling in a hotel room not far from here. Smart and sly. That's me. It'll be a great alibi in case I ever need one."

Did "ever need one" mean that he wasn't planning on killing her? Or did it mean he imagined no one would ever question the governor?

"Look, Allan, there's something important you should know." Her mind raced to find some excuse to stay alive. Give her the break she needed to get away.

He waved the gun at her, and perversely she noted he was wearing a tux. "Shut up. Now that I've found my flash drive—" He pointed the barrel at the monitor as if that said it all. "I don't need to hear anything from you. I've already got a plan. You're going to be killed by whoever's been chasing you. They broke into your condo because you forgot to lock the door and set the alarm.

"*Tsk, tsk,* sweetheart. What a shame." He leveled the gun at her and took aim.

"Wait a second," she begged. "I made a copy of the drive. Kill me and you'll never find it."

Jericho heard the voices coming from Rosie's office and crept closer. He'd been alarmed when he'd arrived back here only to find her front door unlocked and ajar. He definitely remembered Rosie locking it behind him when he'd left.

That's when, on instinct, he'd drawn his service weapon and edged inside the door instead of knocking. Was that Daniels's voice? Absolutely. And Rosie's, too, sounding scared and on the verge of panic.

She'd been right about not coming here. Why hadn't he listened? The only thing he had in his favor now was surprise. That would have to do.

Sneaking up to the office door, Jericho eased it open and peeked inside. Daniels was standing with his back to him, but he was holding a weapon to Rosie's head.

"I said, shut up, bitch." Daniels screamed, clearly out of control. "Lies won't save your traitorous ass. You stole my property. You were going to use it to ruin me.

"If you made a copy and hid it, then where is it? I've had this place searched top to bottom." Daniels rammed the barrel of the gun against Rosie's cheek. "Better make me believe you by telling the truth."

Jericho's anger came up fast and hard. He wanted to shout at Daniels to take his hands off her. It was all he could do to tamp it down and think like the lawman he needed to be.

"Hold it, Daniels," he yelled, jamming the barrel of his 9mm into the man's back. "Drop your weapon. Now!"

Daniels stilled for the moment, but said, "You won't shoot. If you do, your girlfriend here is dead. You'd better drop your gun, sheriff, and we'll have a little conversation."

Nearly blinded by his furor at the man, Jericho fought

his emotions long enough to make the right move. Daniels would have to kill both of them now. It was his only out. But there would be two of them to his one. Jericho figured those odds were in their favor.

At least, he had to give surprise a try. Otherwise, Rosie was dead.

"Okay, Mr. Governor, you've got the upper hand," he said with as casual tone as he could manage. Under his shirt, his muscles bunched and tensed. "I'm going to put my weapon on the floor. Don't be surprised." He kicked the 9mm clear across the room and under a daybed. "See there. Now we can talk."

"Not until you come over here where I can see you," the governor snapped at him. "Carefully. Move to your right. Go stand beside your girlfriend's chair directly in front of me."

Daniels still had his weapon poking into Rosie's temple. Jericho raised his arms slightly, almost offhandedly, and took a docile step to the right.

"Easy there," he told the other man. "I'm moving."

But with his second step, Jericho deliberately stumbled a half a foot closer to Daniels. Surprised and panicked by the sudden move, the governor spun and pulled the trigger without aiming. The shot went wild, off into the ceiling.

Everything happened at once then. Rosie screamed and kicked out at Daniels's gun hand. The weapon flew out of his grip. And in that instant, Jericho was on him.

The two of them were on the floor, grappling and throwing punches. Daniels didn't stand a chance. Not with the superhuman power Jericho's furor provided him.

The son of a bitch had hurt Rosie. He'd planned to kill her! Jericho landed a right and heard Daniels's nose break. Well, let's just see how he likes being hurt.

Battering Daniels's head against the ground, Jericho didn't feel any of the other man's blows and could only think about Rosie. This bastard had been planning on taking away the one woman he loved. Never!

Daniels fought with incredible strength. Still, Jericho remained on top and was numb to any pain. Finally, Jericho edged free enough to ram his knee into the other man's groin. He felt gristle crunching underneath the slacks even as the other man shrieked in pain.

"Hope it hurts like hell, you bastard." A scarlet haze of pure hatred and anger developed in front of Jericho's eyes, as he just kept yelling and punching. Never noticing the other man go limp.

Hitting. Smashing. Landing blow after blow.

Rosie came to her senses and scrambled across the room to get a hold of Allan's gun. She pointed it at the two men on the floor. That was when she saw that Allan wasn't fighting back anymore.

"Jericho, stop." She put the gun down and moved closer when he didn't seem to hear. "Jericho!" she screamed.

Inching closer, she yelled again and got the nerve to shove at his arm. "Please, honey. Don't do this. Stop."

Tears sprang from her eyes and threatened to swamp her, but she kept yelling his name and shoving at his arms and back, desperate to make him understand. *Please, my love. Don't ruin your life—my life—over this piece of garbage.*

At last, Jericho quit swinging and turned to her. Shocked at what she saw, she reached out for him.

Tears rolled down his face, his fury clear but almost spent. Reaching for her, too, he stood and pulled her into his arms.

"Are you okay?" He swiped his face across his shirt-sleeve and choked back an obvious sigh.

His father had been right. There must've been a lot of anger buried in him for all these years.

She looked up into his beloved hazel eyes, now dark green with feeling. "You came back," she managed through her tears. "You came back for me."

"I shouldn't have left. If I'd been a few seconds later…" His words trailed off as she saw the deep emotions swirl across his face.

It thrilled her. Scared her. He seemed so intense. So full of concern for her.

To shake off the strong feelings she didn't know what to do about, she turned back to look at the limp body on the floor. "I hope you didn't kill him. He isn't dead, is he?"

Jericho seemed reluctant to let her go, but in a second she saw the sheriff return to his eyes. He stepped closer to Allan and checked his pulse.

"He's alive," Jericho said with authority. "He's going to live to spend a long time in prison. I can't believe how I missed seeing what a phony he was."

"Everyone missed it. The whole world missed it." She shook her head, heading toward her desk. "I'll call 911 and get an ambulance. Do you think we need to tie him up?"

Jericho reached out and pulled her to a stop. "I'll tie his hands and you can call in a second," he said gently.

"First, I have to apologize to you. I almost lost you. I should've listened when you didn't want to come here. I should've listened when you wanted to leave with me. I…" Again he seemed to choke on his words.

"You didn't know," she said, rubbing uselessly at his sleeve.

He drew in a deep breath. "No. I did know something, if only I'd just paid attention. I knew you loved me and I knew I loved you. That should've been enough."

"You love me?" The adrenaline must be spiking inside her again, because she thought she was hearing things and her whole body began to shake.

"More than anything. It would've killed me to lose you. Literally. I can't…I can't live without you.

"Whatever your name is now, Rosie-Olivia, marry me and change it. In fact, marry me as soon as we clean up here. Today. Tomorrow at the latest. I'm never leaving you again."

The tears started up again and Rosie damned her hormones. But laughing through the rolling rivers of salt on her cheeks, she managed to nod her head.

At last she would know for sure who she was. A woman worthy of respect and love. A woman so full of love for the man who provided it that she thought she might burst.

Epilogue

Pleased with himself for getting the seventy-two-hour waiting period waived and arranging for the justice of the peace on short notice, Jericho stood with his best friend and watched as his new bride talked to his father and brother on the other side of the yard.

"Are we supposed to call her Olivia now that her amnesia is gone?" Clay asked as he poured himself a drink from the temporary refreshment table set up in Jericho's backyard.

Rosie's backyard now, too, Jericho thought with a secret smile. He was simply amazed at how peaceful, how settled he felt since she'd said yes. What a lucky bastard he was.

The governor was recovering from his injuries in the

hospital jail, and many of the questions had already been asked and answered. The worst answer concerned finding the body of the reporter, Mary Beth Caldwell, in the trunk of Rosie's car at the bottom of a ravine. Rosie's testimony, the flash drive and the rest of the pending investigation would put Daniels away for good.

Tilting his head to Clay, Jericho answered, "Mrs. Yates will do for you." A little sarcastic maybe, but then he allowed the smile to show. "Really, she says she prefers Rosie. But she's willing to answer to either one."

Clay nodded as he too looked across the lawn to where Rosie stood. "It's nice your brother's leave isn't over yet so he could be here for your actual wedding. Family is so important at times like this."

Clay sounded so down all of a sudden, not like himself at all.

"You okay?" Jericho asked.

"Yeah. It's just…well, you know I've been writing to my brother, Ryder, in prison. My most recent letters came back as undeliverable."

"What does that mean?" Jericho could see that the news had upset his friend. Maybe a lot more than he was letting on.

"Not sure." Clay looked off at the sunset. "I'm planning on calling the warden to find out. But I've been a little hesitant, knowing it might be something I don't want to hear."

Jericho could understand that. Running instead of standing and listening was something he was real familiar with.

He put his hand on his friend's shoulder. "No matter

what it is, it's better to know the truth. Let me know if you need my help."

Rosie turned to him and their gazes met across the lawn. The thrill ran down his spine, landing squarely in his gut. Would it always be this way? The desperate hunger. The pulse-pounding wave of recognition when he looked her way.

As he walked toward her, he imagined it would probably last a lifetime. When he got close enough to put his arm around her waist, he was positive. This. This exhilaration and breathlessness would never go away.

"So, bro," Fisher began. "You two planning on a hunting trip as a honeymoon?"

Jericho kept his gaze locked with his bride's. "None of your business. Just let us handle the honeymoon."

Moving closer to him, Rosie felt the warmth of her new husband's love clear down to her toes. She stood, basking in both the sun and in the friendship and love she'd found with all these wonderful people.

What an amazing thing it was. Not more than two weeks ago she was a lonely, superficial woman with no family to speak of and no friends. Amazingly, if she'd given it any thought back then, she would've said she was happy. She'd had things, a prominent job and a part-time lover who had power and influence.

But deep down something big had been missing. She hadn't been able to put her finger on it then, just as she hadn't been able to come up with her past over the last days. But she'd kept on reaching—reaching for *love* as she now knew. And for family.

Family. She gazed at her handsome new husband

and then at his loving and gentle father and brother who were chuckling at Jericho's teasing. Well, she had a family now. A better one she never would've found.

Easing her hand over her belly in a protective motion, she reminded herself that there would be one more family member soon. A baby to love and cherish. How lucky could she be?

Smiling at her love, a secret smile that told him all that was in her heart, Rosie Yates decided all was right with the world at last. The sheriff's amnesiac bride had found her mind…her place…her love.

And she meant to hang on to them forever.

* * * * *

Chapter 1

Macy Ward had never imagined that on her wedding day she would be running out of the church instead of walking down the aisle.

But just over a week earlier, she had been drawn out of the church by the sharp crack of gunshots, the harsh squeal of tires followed by the familiar sound of her fiancé's voice shouting for his police cruiser.

Her fiancé, Jericho Yates, the town sheriff and her lifelong friend. Her best friend in all the world and the totally wrong man to marry, she thought again. Her hands tightened on the steering wheel as she shot a glance at her teenage son who was in the passenger seat.

"You ready for this, T.J.?"

He had been listening to his iPod, but at the sound of

her voice, he pulled out one earbud. Tinny, too loud music blared from it as T.J. asked, "Did you want something?"

It was impossible to miss the sullen tones of his voice or the angry set of his jaw.

She had seen a similar irritated expression on the face of T.J.'s biological father, Fisher Yates, as he stood in his dress Army uniform outside the church with his brother—her fiancé. Fisher had looked far more attractive than he should have. As she had raced out into the midst of the bedlam occurring on the steps of the chapel, her gaze had connected with Fisher's stony glare for just a few seconds.

A few seconds too long.

When she had announced to Jericho that they should call off the wedding, she had seen the change in Fisher's gaze.

She wasn't sure if it had been relief at first, although that was what she had thought that it was. But the emotion that followed and lingered there far longer had been something possibly more dangerous.

There was no relief in T.J.'s gaze as he glared at her. Just anger.

"Are you ready for this?" she repeated calmly, shooting him a glance from the corner of her eye as she drove to the center of town.

The loose black T-shirt T.J. wore barely shifted with his indifferent shrug. "Do I have any choice?"

Choice? Did anyone really have many choices in life? she thought, recalling how she would have chosen not to get pregnant by Fisher. Or lose her husband Tim to cancer. Or have a loving and respectful son turn into the troublesome seventeen-year-old hellion.

"You most certainly have choices, T.J. You could have failed your math class or gone to those tutoring sessions. You could have done time in Juvie instead of community service. And now—"

"I'll have to stay out of trouble by working at the ranch since you decided not to marry Sheriff Yates."

"I realized that I was getting married for all the wrong reasons. So I chose not to go ahead with it and I'm glad that I did. It gave Jericho the chance to find someone he truly loves," she said, clasping and unclasping her hands on the wheel as she pulled into a spot in front of the post office on Main Street.

"I don't need another dad," he said, but his words were followed by another shrug as T.J.'s head dropped down. "Not that Jericho isn't a nice guy. He's just not my dad."

Macy killed the engine, cradled her son's chin and applied gentle pressure to urge his head upward. "I know you miss him. I do, too. It's been six long years without him, but he wouldn't want you to still be unhappy."

"And you think working at the ranch with some gnarly surfer dude from California will make me happy?" He jerked away from her touch and wagged one hand in the familiar hang-loose surfer sign.

She dropped her hands into her lap and shook her head, biting back tears and her own anger. As a recreational therapist, she understood the kinds of emotions T.J. was venting with his aggressive behavior. Knew how to try to get him to open up about his feelings.

But as a mother, the attitude was nevertheless frustrating.

"Jewel tells me Joe, Jr. is a great kid, and he's your age. Maybe you'll find that you have something in common."

Without waiting for his reply, she grabbed her purse and rushed out of the car, crossed the street and made a beeline for the door of Miss Sue's. She had promised her boss, Jewel Mayfair, that she would stop to pick up some of the restaurant's famous sticky buns for the kids currently residing at the Hopechest Ranch.

When she reached the door to the restaurant, however, she realized that he was there.

Fisher Yates.

Decorated soldier, Jericho's older brother and unknown to him or anyone else in town, T.J.'s real dad. Only her husband Tim had known, but as honorable as he had been, he had kept the secret to his grave.

The morning that had started out so-so due to T.J.'s moodiness just went to bad. She would have no choice but to acknowledge Fisher on her way to the takeout counter in the back of the restaurant. Especially since he looked up and noticed her standing there. His green-eyed gaze narrowed as he did so and his full lips tightened into a grim line.

He really should loosen up and smile some more, she thought, recalling the Fisher of her youth who had always had a ready grin on his face for her, Tim and Jericho.

Although she couldn't blame him for his seeming reticence around her. She had done her best to avoid him during the entire time leading up to the wedding. Had somehow handled being around him during all the last-minute preparations, being polite but indifferent whenever he was around. It was the only way to protect herself against the emotions that lingered when it came to Fisher.

In the week or so since she and Jericho had parted ways, it had been easier because she hadn't seen Fisher around town all that much and knew it was just a matter of time before he was back on duty and her secret would be safe again.

She ignored the niggle of guilt that Fisher didn't know about T.J. Or that as a soldier, he risked his life with each mission and might not ever know that he had a son. Over the years she had told herself it had been the right decision for both of them. Jericho had told her more than once how happy his older brother was in the army. How it had been the perfect choice for him.

As much as the guilt weighed heavily on her at times, she could not risk any more problems with her son by revealing such a truth now.

T.J. had experienced enough upset in his life lately, and he was the single most important thing in her life. She would do anything to protect him. To see him smile once again.

Which included staying away from Fisher Yates no matter how much she wanted to put things right between them.

* * * * *

Tanner heard the rig roll in around sunset. Smiling, he wandered to the window. Watched as Olivia O'Ballivan climbed out of her Suburban, flung one defiant glance toward the house and started for the barn, the golden retriever trotting along behind her.

Taking his coat and hat down from the peg next to the back door, he put them on and went outside. He was used to being alone, even liked it, but keeping company with Doc O'Ballivan, bristly though she sometimes was, would provide a welcome diversion.

He gave her time to reach the horse Butterpie's stall, then walked into the barn.

The golden retriever came to greet him, all wagging tail and melting brown eyes, and he bent to stroke her soft, sturdy back. "Hey, there, dog," he said.

Sure enough, Olivia was in the stall, brushing Butterpie down and talking to her in a soft, soothing voice that touched something private inside Tanner and made him want to turn on one heel and beat it back to the house.

He'd be damned if he'd do it, though.

This was *his* ranch, *his* barn. Well-intentioned as she was, *Olivia* was the trespasser here, not him.

"She's still very upset," Olivia told him, without turning to look at him or slowing down with the brush.

Shiloh, always an easy horse to get along with, stood contentedly in his own stall, munching away on the feed Tanner had given him earlier. Butterpie, he noted, hadn't touched her supper as far as he could tell.

"Do you know anything at all about horses, Mr. Quinn?" Olivia asked.

He leaned against the stall door, the way he had the day before, and grinned. He'd practically been raised on horseback; he and Tessa had grown up on their grandmother's farm in the Texas hill country, after their folks divorced and went their separate ways, both of them too busy to bother with a couple of kids. "A few things," he said. "And I mean to call you Olivia, so you might as well return the favor and address me by my first name."

He watched as she took that in, dealt with it, decided on an approach. He'd have to wait and see what that turned out to be, but he didn't mind. It was a pleasure just watching Olivia O'Ballivan grooming a horse.

"All right, *Tanner,*" she said. "This barn is a disgrace. When are you going to have the roof fixed? If it snows again, the hay will get wet and probably mold…"

He chuckled, shifted a little. He'd have a crew out

there the following Monday morning to replace the roof and shore up the walls—he'd made the arrangements over a week before—but he felt no particular compunction to explain that. He was enjoying her ire too much; it made her color rise and her hair fly when she turned her head, and the faster breathing made her perfect breasts go up and down in an enticing rhythm. "What makes you so sure I'm a greenhorn?" he asked mildly, still leaning on the gate.

At last she looked straight at him, but she didn't move from Butterpie's side. "Your hat, your boots—that fancy red truck you drive. I'll bet it's customized."

Tanner grinned. Adjusted his hat. "Are you telling me real cowboys don't drive red trucks?"

"There are lots of trucks around here," she said. "Some of them are red, and some of them are new. And *all* of them are splattered with mud or manure or both."

"Maybe I ought to put in a car wash, then," he teased. "Sounds like there's a market for one. Might be a good investment."

She softened, though not significantly, and spared him a cautious half smile, full of questions she probably wouldn't ask. "There's a good car wash in Indian Rock," she informed him. "People go there. It's only forty miles."

"Oh," he said with just a hint of mockery. "*Only* forty miles. Well, then. Guess I'd better dirty up my truck if I want to be taken seriously in these here parts. Scuff up my boots a bit, too, and maybe stomp on my hat a couple of times."

Her cheeks went a fetching shade of pink. "You are

twisting what I said," she told him, brushing Butterpie again, her touch gentle but sure. "I meant…"

Tanner envied that little horse. Wished he had a furry hide, so he'd need brushing, too.

"You *meant* that I'm not a real cowboy," he said. "And you could be right. I've spent a lot of time on construction sites over the last few years, or in meetings where a hat and boots wouldn't be appropriate. Instead of digging out my old gear, once I decided to take this job, I just bought new."

"I bet you don't even *have* any old gear," she challenged, but she was smiling, albeit cautiously, as though she might withdraw into a disapproving frown at any second.

He took off his hat, extended it to her. "Here," he teased. "Rub that around in the muck until it suits you."

She laughed, and the sound—well, it caused a powerful and wholly unexpected shift inside him. Scared the hell out of him and, paradoxically, made him yearn to hear it again.

* * * * *

Discover how this rugged rancher's wanderlust is tamed in time for a merry Christmas, in A STONE CREEK CHRISTMAS. *In stores December 2008.*

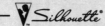
SPECIAL EDITION™

**FROM *NEW YORK TIMES*
BESTSELLING AUTHOR**

LINDA LAEL
MILLER

A STONE CREEK
CHRISTMAS

Veterinarian Olivia O'Ballivan finds the animals
in Stone Creek playing Cupid between her and
Tanner Quinn. Even Tanner's daughter, Sophie,
is eager to play matchmaker. With everyone
conspiring against them and the holiday season
fast approaching, Tanner and Olivia may just get
everything they want for Christmas after all!

*Available December 2008
wherever books are sold.*

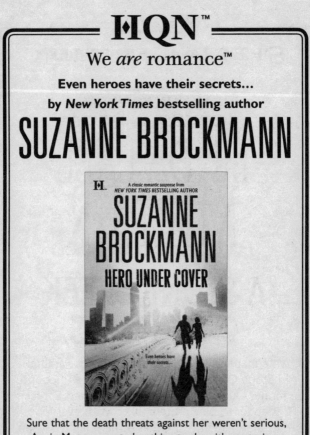

SPECIAL EDITION™

Kate's Boys

MISTLETOE AND MIRACLES

by *USA TODAY* bestselling author
MARIE FERRARELLA

Child psychologist Trent Marlowe couldn't believe his eyes when Laurel Greer, the woman he'd loved and lost, came to him for help. Now a widow, with a troubled boy who wouldn't speak, Laurel needed a miracle from Trent...and a brief detour under the mistletoe wouldn't hurt, either.

Available in December wherever books are sold.

REQUEST YOUR FREE BOOKS!

2 FREE NOVELS PLUS 2 FREE GIFTS!

Silhouette® Romantic

SUSPENSE

Sparked by Danger, Fueled by Passion!

YES! Please send me 2 FREE Silhouette® Romantic Suspense novels and my 2 FREE gifts (gifts are worth about $10). After receiving them, if I don't wish to receive any more books, I can return the shipping statement marked "cancel." If I don't cancel, I will receive 4 brand-new novels every month and be billed just $4.24 per book in the U.S. or $4.99 per book in Canada, plus 25¢ shipping and handling per book plus applicable taxes, if any*. That's a savings of at least 15% off the cover price! I understand that accepting the 2 free books and gifts places me under no obligation to buy anything. I can always return a shipment and cancel at any time. Even if I never buy another book from Silhouette, the two free books and gifts are mine to keep forever.

240 SDN EEX6   340 SDN EEYJ

Name _____ (PLEASE PRINT)

Address _____ Apt. #

City _____ State/Prov. _____ Zip/Postal Code

Signature (if under 18, a parent or guardian must sign)

Mail to the **Silhouette Reader Service:**

IN U.S.A.: P.O. Box 1867, Buffalo, NY 14240-1867
IN CANADA: P.O. Box 609, Fort Erie, Ontario L2A 5X3

Not valid to current subscribers of Silhouette Romantic Suspense books.

Want to try two free books from another line?
Call 1-800-873-8635 or visit www.morefreebooks.com.

* Terms and prices subject to change without notice. N.Y. residents add applicable sales tax. Canadian residents will be charged applicable provincial taxes and GST. Offer not valid in Quebec. This offer is limited to one order per household. All orders subject to approval. Credit or debit balances in a customer's account(s) may be offset by any other outstanding balance owed by or to the customer. Please allow 4 to 6 weeks for delivery. Offer available while quantities last.

Your Privacy: Silhouette is committed to protecting your privacy. Our Privacy Policy is available online at www.eHarlequin.com or upon request from the Reader Service. From time to time we make our lists of customers available to reputable third parties who may have a product or service of interest to you. If you would prefer we not share your name and address, please check here. ☐

SRS08R

Harlequin® Historical
Historical Romantic Adventure!

THE MISTLETOE WAGER

Christine Merrill

Harry Pennyngton, Earl of Anneslea,
is surprised when his estranged wife,
Helena, arrives home for Christmas.
Especially when she's intent on
divorce! A festive house party
is in full swing when the guests
are snowed in, and Harry and
Helena find they are together
under the mistletoe....

*Available December 2008
wherever books are sold.*

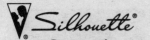

Romantic

SUSPENSE

COMING NEXT MONTH

#1539 BACKSTREET HERO—Justine Davis
Redstone, Incorporated
When Redstone executive Lilith Mercer is nearly injured in two suspicious accidents, her boss calls in security expert Tony Alvera. But the street-tough, too-attractive *younger* agent is the last man Lilith wants protecting her as she faces her tarnished past. They get closer to the truth, and find that danger—and love—are hiding in plain sight.

#1540 SOLDIER'S SECRET CHILD—Caridad Piñeiro
The Coltons: Family First
They'd shared one night of passion eighteen years ago, but Macy Ward had never told anyone that Fisher Yates was the father of her son, T.J. Now Fisher is back in town, and when T.J. disappears, Macy turns to him for help. Will their search for their son reveal the passion they've been denying all these years?

#1541 MERRICK'S ELEVENTH HOUR—Wendy Rosnau
Spy Games
Adolf Merrick—code name Icis—has discovered a mole in the NSA Onyxx Agency, which has allowed his nemesis to stay one step ahead. In a plot to capture his enemy, Merrick kidnaps the man's wife—who mysteriously has his own dead wife's face! With the clock ticking and the stakes high, Merrick is in a race against time for the truth.

#1542 PROTECTED IN HIS ARMS—Suzanne McMinn
Haven
Amateur psychic Marysia O'Hurley figures her powers are the real deal when U.S. Marshal Gideon Brand enlists her help. The reluctant allies embark on a roller-coaster ride to rescue a little girl, with killers one step behind them. Even as they dodge bullets, will they find passion in each other's arms?

SRSCNMBPA1108